OMG
Christmas Tree

Contents

Chapter 1

Megan

I was destined to be a disappointment.

"I know Christmas is in four days," I told my mother into the phone for the second time in as many minutes. "The reason I'm working is *because* it's the holidays. Everyone wants the next few days off for vacation."

"And *you* never get one. Not even a measly few days to see your family."

Heaping spoonful of guilt, anyone?

"We have an event at the cafe tonight," I responded. "Running special events puts me one step closer to store manager." I glanced over my shoulder, hoping nobody heard me. I didn't want to sound desperate.

"Can't a coffee shop shut down for a week? There are plenty of places for people to get coffee in Chicago."

A coffee grinder buzzed, cutting any reply short. Funny, I was the one with my thumb on the GRIND button.

"Sorry, can't hear!" I shouted, scrunching my shoulder toward my ear to hold the slim phone steady. Naturally, it tumbled onto the counter face down into a puddle of peppermint creamer.

My coworker Cam reached across me and shut the grinder off. "Take your break, Megan."

"The gaming group will be here in twenty—"

"How about now." Cam's usual soft brown eyes blackened.

"Got it." I pinched the phone from the counter and wiped the screen against my apron along the *Drip* name and logo. "I have this under control."

Cam said nothing. Simply looked at the grinder in front of me.

Empty. I'd been grinding nothing but bean dust and generational angst.

Sigh. I zipped into the back room.

"My wedding, Megan," Mom was saying through the phone. "You missed my wedding."

I switched the phone to my other ear, Silly me. Like my right ear would suddenly make this conversation any easier.

"Mom, you know I would have gone if—"

"You didn't have to work." She filled in for me. "That's always the case. Well, I'm telling you the truth. It upset me. And your grandmother. And Stu. Stu is still upset."

I shut my eyes, but her words seeped through. "I'm sorry I missed your vows with Stu." What sort of name was Stu, anyhow? *Short for Stuart,* my brain reminded. Shut up, brain! "You gave me two days' notice. I couldn't get to Wisconsin that fast. Not when the work schedule already went up."

The line went quiet. On the other side of the door, coffee grinding (actual beans this time; Cam had that down) and customers chatting offered familiar comfort.

"It's been a tough few years." Mom's tone softened. "I miss my baby. I want you to see how far we've come. How happy I am with Stu. I want you to be part of this Christmas."

"I know." The printed shift schedule on the bulletin board blurred before my eyes. Tears? Now, at work? I wiped my cheek. "I miss Dad."

"Oh, honey. Me too. He'll always be with us. Always."

Four years since we lost him and some days it felt like yesterday. The holidays brought it all back. All the feels.

"I wish we'd had one last Christmas in the house." I cringed at my own words. The things that fell out of my mouth sometimes...

"It made sense to move in with Stu since I'm retired." Her words became clipped, her tone less sympathetic. "The house sold quickly. That's good news to most people."

I wanted to hold on to our house the way it always had been. Wishful thinking.

"Your father would have wanted you to spend the holidays with your family."

Back to my time off, or lack of. Guilt: double shot, no whip, topped off with more guilt.

She wasn't wrong. Dad would have wanted us all together for the holidays, including my brother, Derek. He lived in Seattle, working in tech. As hard as Dad worked, he'd always made time for us during the holidays.

But it wouldn't be our family. Stu's adult children were coming in for a big dinner at his—his and Mom's—house. His kids had careers in podiatry and particle physics. Grinding coffee beans couldn't compete with smashing atoms.

My dream? *Hoping* to be a coffee shop manager.

"I wouldn't ask if it wasn't important to me." Mom's voice thickened with emotion.

She'd already stirred me up with the Dad stuff. When it came to him, I couldn't say no. The work excuse wouldn't hold up. I owed my mom to be with her this holiday.

I grabbed the staff schedule off the board. "I'll give it the old Campbell Can-Do."

It's what Dad would have done.

· ❤ · ❤ · ❤ · ❤ · ❤ ·

I owed two coworkers coverage any day they needed for the next six months. *Brain: add Learn negotiating skills to my To-Do list.*

Three days until Christmas and I was due back the day after the holiday. Now that Mom was with Stu, she lived so far north their backyard edged the Wisconsin state line.

I headed out with my car's backseat only partly filled by a suitcase and a small bag of gifts. Not five minutes later, my phone rang in the seat beside me. No Bluetooth in this old thing, so I poked the speaker icon without looking.

"Megan, it's your mother."

"Do you call Derek this often?"

"Did I tell you he's coming? Derek just got a last minute flight."

Of course, he'd be there. He probably kept his long-planned visit a surprise with a story about last minute tickets. He knew it would delight Mom. Derek was so predictable. And reliable. Things I strived for, but usually fell short.

"I'm glad I caught you," she went on through the speaker. "If you could pick up a tree for us on the way in, that would be so helpful. Sawyer's Tree Farm. You'll see it a mile from our exit."

Brake lights strobed ahead in a seemingly endless red ribbon. "I'm sorry, what? I thought you said something about a tree."

"The tree farm is on your way to the house. If you could pick one up for us on your way in."

A real live Christmas tree. From a tree farm. A tradition my family never participated in. Why now? "You want me to get you a Christmas tree?"

"After our weekend trip to Lake Geneva and getting settled after the kitchen upgrade, we haven't had time to put up decorations. The tree will be easy. Up here, they do it all for you. They'll carry the tree to your car and tie it to the roof."

Right. A whole tree tied to my roof. Perfectly normal.

"The tree is going in the front room," she continued. "Our home has a two-story foyer, so we can fit a nice-sized tree."

I bristled at *our home*. Time to muster the family Campbell Can-Do attitude. "Okay."

"You have enough money, don't you? We'll pay you back of course."

"Yes, Mom. I have enough money for a single Christmas tree."

Never mind I had no clue how much a real tree cost. Or an artificial one. My own fake tree came from a garage sale complete with someone else's homemade ornaments, my fave being a *Mery Christmus 1987* stuffed sachet with a cross-eyed cross-stitched puppy.

Also, never mind my bank balance held a decidedly unimpressive amount of money. I paid my rent on time and I never went hungry. I was doing just fine, and with that promotion to store manager, I'd be even better.

"I won't keep you. Stay safe on the road." Mom ended the call without extended fanfare. Ever the efficient woman from her career as a nurse.

Mom, retired. Taking weekend trips and renovating a kitchen? Wild. Our old kitchen never changed for the entirety of my childhood. The counters bore scars from a generation of holiday baking and family dinners. The wallpaper peeled in predictable places, with my brother's and my height marks penciled in beside the patio door.

Traffic inched forward. Me and half the population of Chicago headed out of the city for the holidays. If only I were going home.

Chapter 2

Nick

"**H**ey, Nick, what's up?"

I held up my hand for Ethan Sawyer's fist bump.

"I expected you at least a week ago," Ethan said.

"Yeah, yeah." I shoved my own gloveless hand back into my coat pocket. "I meant to swing by, but life is a little...different this year. Besides, I knew you'd save a tree for us."

Ethan, bearded and wearing a heavy red-and-black checked coat, called across the lot to his also-bearded brother. "We still got the Benningtons' tree?"

His brother Rob ran a credit card through a handheld reader. A family circled around him holding their chosen tree, big and round at the bottom with a skinny, crooked top. A pretty busted-looking tree if you asked me, but the little girl hopping up and down didn't seem to mind. Rob handed back the card and looked over at us. "It's almost Christmas, man. We have to sell what we have."

Mild panic shot through me. I turned back to Ethan. "You don't have our tree?" The Sawyer Tree Farm always kept one of their best—at least ten feet—for our family.

Ethan hefted a bundle of firewood onto a pyramid stack. "I got here five minutes ago. Rob's been handling the sales."

With the family now walking off, Rob tucked in earbuds and jammed to music only he could hear. I marched over. "Hey." No answer as Rob air-drummed a solo. "Hey. Rob!"

Rob swiveled toward me, still rocking to his own theme. "Sorry, man. Business picks up close to Christmas. Everybody coming in last minute."

Last minute. I heard it in my mother's voice this time. A pang hit me right in the gut. This year of all years I couldn't afford to slack. Stupid me figured the tree was the last of the worries. The Sawyer Farm always had our back. I grew up with these guys. My parents knew their middle names and used them liberally when we boys got in trouble.

"You know we've got the mayor's charity event Christmas Eve," I told Ethan, who'd followed me over. "It's my responsibility to get the tree."

"Hey." Ethan's gruff voice softened. "How's your mom doing, anyhow?"

"Good. We think the radiation will work." I silently cursed the tumors plaguing her body. One more year left on her mayoral term and cancer tried to take her down. We wouldn't let it. I sighed, taking in the trees nobody else wanted. Not a great selection.

Rob let out a breath in a white puff against the brisk December air. "We hung onto one for you, but figured if you wanted it, you would have come by now. I sold the tree ten minutes ago."

"Ten minutes?" I scanned the lot. "They're gone?"

"Yeah. I tied that monster to a joke of a sedan. Twenty bucks says it won't make it home without a flat tire."

Ethan elbowed his brother. "Jerk. The tree will fall off the roof if you're the one who tied it."

"Nope. I tied that sucker tight."

Their bickering faded. All I heard: *ten minutes ago* and *won't make it home.*

"It's been real." I tipped my chin up at the brothers as my send-off. Traitors.

I jumped into my truck and threw it in reverse, nearly taking down a tree that gave Charlie Brown's a run at most pathetic pine. I shifted into drive and turned out of the lot, headed toward town. Somebody packing a ten-foot tree onto a dinky car wouldn't chance the highway.

With last night's temperature drop, the snowy roads had turned slick with ice. This was stupid. I was chasing some stranger who bought the tree I should have picked up weeks ago. I pounded my fist against the wheel. *Don't cancel the benefit. I'll take care of everything.* My own words haunted me.

A giant spruce loomed ahead on the left side of the road. I just needed a chainsaw and the cover of night—

I hit the brakes. My all-wheel snow tires did the job and brought me to stop. I checked my mirror — not a car in sight behind me. Ahead, a car angled into the ditch. A giant Christmas tree hung lopsided off the roof.

·❤·❤·❤·❤·❤·

I pulled to the side of the road behind the ditch-bound car and jumped out of my truck. Someone could be inside, hurt, unless this car had been sitting here awhile. But given the size of the tree and Rob's story about the sad sedan, this had to be the same car that just left the Sawyer lot.

I approached the car. Through the driver's side window, a person appeared hunched over a cell phone.

I knocked on the window. "You okay in there? I can help."

Snow and exhaust streaked the window. A mechanical whir sounded and died, but the glass didn't budge. The door opened instead.

A woman stepped out. A twenty-something-ish, puffy-coated woman with pale skin instantly turning rosy from the crisp wind. A thin silver hoop circled one side of her nose and long dark curls fell from her knit cap. The cap had one of those fuzz balls on top.

Her eyes widened at the sight of me. "Oh, hi. Thank you so much for stopping."

My jaw fell open. It actually hinged open like some Neanderthal mouth-breather.

I snapped it shut. Those traitors. The Sawyer brothers neglected to mention a key detail. That person they sold my tree to happened to be gorgeous.

She held up her phone. "I'm still trying to find the number for my car insurance company. When I switched phones this year, the number must not have saved to the cloud. And of course, the tree would decide to slide off the roof in the center of absolutely nothing. Can you believe they wanted me to get them a tree? I mean, really?" She looked at me with expectation.

Okay, so, shaken up. "Are you okay? You're not hurt?"

"Oh. No, I'm fine. I'm annoyed, is all." She sighed. "I have one bar of connectivity to the outside world. And I'm not about to call my mom."

Her dilemma hit home more than I cared to admit. "Okay, so you're not hurt. Your car is...stuck in a ditch." I peeked around to the other side of the car where the tree hung loose from its ties. "Where'd you get this tree?"

"The lot down the road. Sawyers."

Confirmed. "Friggin' Rob."

"What?"

"Nothing. They did a terrible job tying this." Rob must have been distracted. Kind of like how I was distracted by this flustered, very pretty woman who clearly needed help. I sized up her car. "Doesn't seem safe to tie it back. They should've known back at the lot you couldn't get this home with what you're driving."

She visibly flinched. "Look. I'm doing the best I can. Do you have a signal? I can try calling roadside help from your phone."

Luckily, I had a truck. And if luck was truly on my side, this tree would come home with me.

I gave her what I hoped was an understanding nod. "I have an idea." I pointed back toward my ride. "How about I take the tree off your hands? I'll pay you cash, and we'll get you out of this ditch." I flashed the reliable Bennington smile, the one that melted hearts and won votes (depending on the Bennington).

She squinted at me, tilting her head as if noticing me for the first time. "I'm keeping the tree, but I'll take your offer of delivering it to my parent's—Mom's—I mean, to...the place I'm going to for Christmas."

Delivery? Okay, she clearly felt agitated and misheard me. Her car ran off the road—understood. This would take more finesse. I held out my hand. "I'm Nick."

She eyed it, scrunched her eyebrows, and shook with a puffy knit mitten. "Megan."

"Hi, Megan." Her name sounded nice as I spoke it out loud. I glanced toward the tree. "How about we circle back to the tree farm and get a size more suitable for you."

"I picked this tree for a reason." Her response came quick and firm. "This is the tree I want."

Okay. "I'll double what you paid for it."

"What? Why?"

I took out my wallet and flipped through the bills. We always paid the Sawyers in cash. "I've got it all here. Name your price."

"Name my price?"

She clearly thought I'd chucked my brain across two-lanes into the pasture. Still, I had her. She stood quiet, lost in thought.

"No." She folded her arms. "I'm not giving you this tree. And I resent how you think I don't know what size tree is *suitable*." She shoved her phone into her pocket and headed for the front end of the tree, yanking the branches.

Plan B or C needed to happen quick. "I'll help you get the tree where you're going." Not at all what I wanted to say.

She let out an exasperated noise as pine needles tore from the branch onto her mittens, sticking out like a buzz-cut on a porcupine. "I would be grateful for the help. Thank you."

Grateful meant a step toward flexible. I had this. "Let's make sure the branches aren't damaged already." A bent-up tree wouldn't look so great in the mayor's mansion for the charity event. The mansion was designated a historic site—our family didn't live there. Right now, they had one small tree in a front hall. I needed a large tree for the ballroom.

I grabbed for the trunk and jiggled it free from the bush. Megan watched a foot away, so I flashed her a grin over my shoulder as I stepped back to swing the trunk my way.

My boot slipped. One small patch of ice and everything fell off kilter. Scrambling, I windmilled my arms, stumbled back, then forward, tripping over my own feet and landing face-first into the pine.

Megan gasped. "Are you okay?"

My face would heal. My dignity? Nope.

I shook myself free and stood like nothing happened. "I'll untie the rest of the tree." Yup. Plenty of untying to do. Yessiree.

"You'd think they'd salt the roads here in Wisconsin."

The air of contempt in her tone came so distinct I tasted it bitter on my tongue.

"We're still in Illinois, you know. Is that where you're going? Wisconsin?" If so, depending where in Wisconsin, this would be a long day.

"Practically. Crystal Cove is the town. I had to look it up on the freaking map."

I laughed. "Yeah. We're far up here all right."

Moooo

Megan shrieked. "Is that a cow?"

I looked up. "Sure is." The cow must have wandered over for the free show. A thin metal fence separated the animal from the ditch.

She stepped back. Like the cow would hop the fence and, what? Ask for a ride?

"It's a miracle they let us exist here with them," I said. As the ropes fell away, a sticker on the windshield caught my eye. A City of Chicago parking permit. "Ah, a city girl. Makes sense."

She was right behind me now. "It makes sense a city girl wouldn't know what size tree to buy?"

Exactly. But I couldn't say that. "Your boots aren't exactly made for snow." Skinny heels, shiny black leather. They'd probably never touched a country road.

"Unlike your boots that kept you steady?" Her eyes sparked with delight.

I felt my cheeks flush. She had me there. "Point taken."

I let the tree roll off the car fully to the ground.

Megan watched as I dragged the tree to the truck bed. *Come on, hero vibes. Show strong.*

I hoisted the tree into the truck. This thing was no joke. It would fit the event space in the grand ballroom, but the *grand* in Crystal Cove's ballroom was limited. Any bigger and this beast would dent the ceiling.

The tree now safely secured inside my truck bed, I turned back to Megan. Her nose shone as pink as her cheeks. "Do you have the address?"

She checked her phone again and told me the address. I knew the area well. A country road with garages as big the houses, to larger, newer homes with professional landscaping and long winding drives. "Roger that. I'll follow you."

She snort-laughed, covering her mouth with her mitten. "Sorry. You said Roger that. It's something my dad—" She stopped. "My dad said that." Her gaze drifted to the road silent of passing cars.

She looked back with an expression I couldn't figure out. A mix of fatigue and maybe some shock from going off the road. Could be dreading the upcoming holiday. Or maybe that was me. Probably she felt annoyed her tree had arrowed into a bush with a cow laughing at us on the other side.

Either way, she was out of sorts. "I happen to live in Crystal Cove myself," I told her. "If you'd like, you can follow me."

Her shoulders eased. "That would be fantastic."

Megan's smile was back, and dang it if I didn't get a burst of energy from it. "Now, let's get this car out of the ditch."

Chapter 3

Megan

Life was much improved now that a nefarious conifer no longer clung to my car's roof. Bonus, the guy coming to my aid wasn't a serial killer. Serial killers didn't say things like *Roger that.* Nick was cute. So cute I nearly gawked at him speechless until I remembered to thank him for stopping. He even had an honest to goodness dimple when he grinned.

Not that I was swayed by dimples. I liked arty guys with chiseled features. Broody types who dressed in black and gray. Nick wore a pricey brand waterproof parka the color of an evergreen with a coordinating plaid scarf. The guy looked practically *festive.*

Ahead of me, Nick's truck slowed within sight of a stop sign. He'd started breaking earlier than he needed to driving a truck with those winter tires. My own tires slid as I gently pressed the brakes. Oh, right. He slowed early for my sake. Thoughtful.

A sign with Crystal Cove in retro cursive announced our arrival. Greenery hung along the edges of the sign with red bows shouting from the top corners. Beyond the sign, the street lit up. Okay, maybe I was a sucker, but I gasped. Even in early evening, the town—it looked magical. White lights wound around spindly tree branches and street lampposts. More lights hung in narrow vertical rows against brick building exteriors and spilled out of flower boxes stuffed with holiday greens. Crystal Cove played the holiday game and played it well.

We shot out the other end of Main Street to a stretch of road with nothing notable, the light fading to gradually deepening darkness. Nick's truck made a right, a left, then another right. I'd have been lost on my own.

The truck slowed and I tapped my brakes, wincing at the fishtail from my tires. *Stupid unsalted country roads. Stupid nearly-bald tires.*

Nick turned into a driveway. We were here. I gaped at the house. Seriously, Mom lived here? With Stu and what other family? This place could eat my childhood home with a side of graham crackers and milk.

Nick eased up to the garage, his truck taking up the whole middle of the driveway. Something I realized as I careened straight toward it.

Too much momentum. I steered right and slid toward a mass of snow piled along the edge of the driveway. The snowdrift accepted my front end with a foreboding *squnch*. Like a snow-mound padlock clicking into place.

Well, I'd made it.

I stared at the house. The house stared back. Not a mansion or anything but large and modern. Not at all what I expected.

Knuckles rapped against my window, sending me jumping in my seat. "You getting out?" Nick's muffled voice carried through.

Now or never. Could I choose never?

I opened the door and the cold nipped at my skin.

"Nice place." Nick stood broad-shouldered like a corn-fed hay baler. That's what country guys did, right? Baled hay? Loaded pine trees from truck beds?

The house loomed over us. "It's kind of shocking." I pointed to the house next door, set farther back from the road. "Who needs a four-car garage?"

"Boats? ATVs? Lots of people have extra storage garages up here."

Derp. Of course, he was right. But I could dwell on my obvious ignorance about sprawling homes in the borderlands on my own time. "Listen, thank you so much for bringing the tree here. I'm sure I would have gotten lost." He probably expected a tip. I only had ten bucks cash on me. Ten bucks tip wasn't horrible, right? I rummaged through my purse. "Here." I handed him the crisp bill.

He leaned against the back of the truck, an unreadable grin on his face. "How about you keep your ten spot. I can still take this tree off your hands. There's a big box store down the road who sells trees."

"You drove all the way to Stu—to my family's house." Ugh. Still couldn't get used to saying that. "Why are you trying to convince me to give up the tree?"

"Are you hosting a party?"

"What? My brother's coming in from Seattle."

"So, you, your brother, and your parents, and this magnificent pine?"

"This pine *is* magnificent. My...family is going to love it."

He crossed his arms, scrutinizing the house. "Step family?"

"Something like that." Screamingly obvious. *Petulant Twenty-Something Avoids New Step-Dad at Christmas — next on Your Basic Millennial Stereotype.* "We always had an artificial tree. This year my mom asked for a real tree and tasked me with bringing it. It's our first Christmas here."

Unless Mom bought out the ornament section at Target, I had no idea what else we could put on the tree. Our childhood ornaments would barely cover half of this thing.

Nick didn't say anything and we both sort of stood there looking at the house. I would need to go inside eventually.

"Did you know Crystal Cove was named the number two holiday destination in the state, second only to Chicago?" Nick suddenly asked.

"By what, Small Town Quarterly magazine?"

He named a major travel publication. *Double derp.*

"You said you grew up with a fake tree. What happened to it?"

"I...I don't know." I didn't know what happened to any of our old stuff. Mom had threatened Derek and me to pack our old bedrooms and the garage or our remaining stuff would land in a giant rented Dumpster. Eventually, she'd told us the movers put it all in the moving truck and we could sort our boxes later. Whether she'd done the same for Dad's things, well, I didn't know. Because I hadn't asked.

I looked up to find Nick watching me. I sensed pity in his eyes and hated it. Whatever mess I'd made of the years after Dad, I didn't need Nick's sympathy.

The front door to the house opened. "Megan. I didn't hear you drive in." Mom ducked back inside and reappeared wearing a heavy cardigan. "I had headphones in doing my daily meditations."

Wow, retirement had done one over on her. Not in a bad way just... different.

Mom stepped with care down the shoveled front walk in slippers with firm soles. "You didn't tell me you were bringing someone. Hello."

"He's not—"

"I'm Nick." He held a hand out to her.

She beamed with all the wattage of Crystal Cove's downtown holiday scene.

"He's helping me with the tree. From Sawyer's." Mom didn't need to know I ended up in a ditch or the likelihood I needed four new tires with no funds to cover it.

"You're a Sawyer boy?" Mom asked. "How delightful."

Nick looked over at me, and I telegraphed AGREE in bold font.

"I'm not a Sawyer. I'm a Bennington."

I pelted him with non-verbal exclamations. *How could you!*

"Bennington." Mom blinked rapidly. "Mayor Bennington's son? Oh, dear, how is your family?"

"My mom, she's holding up well," Nick answered. "Really putting up a fight. Dad is hanging in there in his own way."

What was happening? Mayor? My mom knew his family after a measly, however-many months living here?

Mom focused on Nick. "I didn't know you helped at the tree farm. What a great way to serve the community." She peered over the truck bed. "That's quite a tree."

"Isn't it great?" I circled behind Nick and unlatched the rear door. Branches shot forward like a pine-filled trap set free.

Mom jerked back. "Oh, dear."

Nick adjusted the branches so they appeared more contained. Slightly. "If you think the tree is too large, I can drive this one back and find you a smaller one."

I stepped in front of him. "This one is perfect. It goes in the two-story window, right Mom?"

"Well..."

The front door opened again. Stu strolled out in a zip-up thermal, dark jeans, and work boots. If you looked up *Retiree, examples of* online, you'd see Stu's picture. Ruddy-skinned with salt and pepper hair. He was the guy who enjoyed a steak and potatoes dinner and a Sunday ride on a pontoon boat. "Nick Bennington. Well, look at you. Helping out at the Sawyer farm this year?"

"Stu?" Nick looked from Stu to me, from me to Stu. "Your stepdad is Stu Krueger?"

Small towns turned out to be barrels of fun. Brimming-full barrels. "Looks like it."

Stu pulled Nick into a one-armed hug. Any second now they'd take up arm wrestling. "Woo, this here is a fine tree. And big." Stu turned to me, thankfully sparing me a physical greeting. "Megan, good to see you. Ah, what's that? Looks like you've got a nail in your nose."

"Ha-ha," I spoke the laugh. "Just a nose ring."

At least he liked the tree. Hopefully, it would grow on Mom, too. If the tree made her happy, then the hassle of bringing it here...well, I could figure out if it was worth it once we made our way inside.

When I didn't respond, Stu moved his attention to the truck bed. "Thanks for picking this up."

I opened my mouth to say *No big deal,* even though it had turned into a bit of a deal. Only Stu wasn't talking to me. He was talking to Nick. I pressed my lips together suppressing an outburst. *I* bought the tree. With all my cash and tips, *thankyouverymuch.*

Nick smiled like a crazed politician (or her son). "Are you sure? It's a big tree. If you're intent on keeping it..."

I swore Nick's neck hairs stood on end. The air charged with subtext rich enough for a literary novel.

Stu tugged on a tree branch, perhaps testing its strength. "Of course, we're keeping it. We may keep it through Valentine's." He winked at my mother.

Nick didn't want us to have the tree. A curious situation. His *insistence* in wanting this tree for himself was curious indeed.

Nick had secrets.

"Little help carrying it inside?" Stu asked Nick.

Nick avoided looking at me. "Sure." He slid the tree halfway off the truck bed, then crouched and hoisted the unruly pine up and out with near expertise. I almost believed he worked at Sawyer's and I'd made that part up.

As the guys hauled the tree into the house, Mom hugged me. "I'm so glad you're here. I know it was a sacrifice for you."

Sacrifice sounded too strong a word until I remembered all the shifts I promised to cover. "I'm glad to be here too. You must be freezing." I grabbed my bags from the car, noting how wholeheartedly the snow pile accepted its newly parked guest. At least here, parking was free.

Mom held open the door to the house for me. "Nick comes from a great family. Mayor Bennington is making our little town so special. We're the number two holiday destination in the state."

"So I've heard."

"Our little town" used to be a town sixty miles south of here. Crystal Cove didn't belong to me. And I wasn't sure I belonged here.

Inside, the house smelled like a forest. Looked like one too, with the foyer covered in green branches.

No matter. "This tree is awesome. I love it, don't you?"

"It sure is...awesome." Mom's tone said *Campbell Can-do* at full force. Making *do* with the situation.

Stu parted a few middle branches and shined a mini flashlight at the trunk, mumbling to himself like an amateur arborist. "A strong tree. This'll last awhile if we keep her watered."

I got the feeling Stu didn't decorate much.

Mom clasped her hands. "We don't have a tree stand. That old fake tree didn't spark the joy it used to, so I Marie Kondo-ed it right out."

Who was this woman? My mother, not Marie Kondo.

"I can pick one up for you." Nick, standing smack-dab in the center of things, seemed to have a solution for everything.

"No, *I'll* get the stand." He'd likely come back with a smaller tree and weasel Stu into a trade.

"Won't your tires slip on the icy roads?" Nick looked at me and deliberately glanced to my mom.

"You didn't have trouble driving here, did you?" Mom's Worry-Mode had activated.

Nick shot my mom a look of measured concern. "Coming into town, the roads are slick. Megan had a little trouble on the road. That's how I found her."

Mom gasped. "Oh, Megan, are you okay? Did you go into a ditch? Stu, did you hear? Megan went into the ditch. And, Nick, you found her?"

I cast Nick a stony look. Me in a ditch was not his business to share. "I'm fine, Mom. Yes, Nick helped me." I wasn't sure why he was here, explaining it all. "And thank you. For the ditch rescue."

Nick grinned. "My pleasure."

"We can't ask you to do anything more," Mom said to Nick. "Stu can pick up what we need for the tree."

I raised my hand for emphasis. "I am perfectly capable of finding a tree stand." Something I should have considered when I bought the tree. I could fix this. I still had my coat on. "I'll go."

I excused myself, walked out the door, and marched over to my car. A little bit of GPS and some gumption, and Merry Christmas to all of us.

The engine revved, but the car stayed put. Ugh, the snow bank. I'd need a shovel.

Knocking sounded on my window. Again, really? I would power down the window, but the window didn't work when it was cold. "I'm a little stuck is all," I said through the glass. *Sigh.* Fine. I got out.

Mom and Stu huddled together behind Nick. Mom nosed forward. "Megan, your car looks dented."

Great. Exactly what I needed.

Stu knelt by the rear tire. "These are awfully worn. Best we change the tires out. I can take your car into the shop tomorrow."

"The tires are *fine*." Even as I said it, the lie tasted sharp. I looked at my car. Dirty, damaged, and kicking its feet up into snowbank like it deserved a vacation. The car was stuck. Like a metaphor for my life.

Nick looked at me with a slightly apologetic expression. "My truck has winter tires. It's a straight shot to the home improvement store—easy trip, I don't mind. Maybe Megan can come along? Help me to pick out what you need."

Oh, my mother loved this. She was winking at me through her excitement. Writing the fanfic herself.

"Me? At a home improvement store?" My arsenal of apartment remedies were limited to batteries, a hammer, and duct tape.

"I promise, I'll make this up to you," Nick said to me in a low tone.

Stu handed him a few crisp bills. "Keep the rest for gas and your time."

Nick accepted the money. "Sure thing." He turned his attention to me. "Ready?"

I nodded, reluctantly. To be honest, I was mostly curious why this Nick Bennington made me any sort of promise at all.

Chapter 4

Nick

Once in my truck with Megan, I knew I needed to give her an explanation.

She clicked in and spun to look at me. "You're the mayor's son?"

I sighed. "I am."

"How do you know my mom?"

"I don't. My family's in the local news a lot. It's an active community. Stu I've known forever."

"You're not telling me something. Why do you want my tree?"

The way she called it her tree made me smile. Time to come clean. "So, I messed up. The Sawyers save a tree for the mayoral benefit and I didn't pick it up in time. The tree is supposed to go in the historic mayor's mansion ballroom for the charity party. Which I also need to plan. For Christmas Eve."

Megan blinked at me. "You said *need to plan.* Does that mean you haven't started?"

"The planning was *started.*" My defenses kicked in, but the truth lay bare as the ballroom I'd failed to decorate. "The mayor's office started the planning. They handle the guest list and catering."

"But trusted you for the tree."

For some reason. "The mayor is supposed to hand-select the tree and the decorations. Seemed easy enough." I even sounded like a loser saying it. The task was easy and I still failed. "This year, it's, she couldn't. I told my parents I'd help and now...I'm in over my head."

"Your mom is sick?"

My throat tightened. "Cancer. She's doing okay, but her treatment and appointments take a lot of time, so my dad is a little overwhelmed. The doctor said she needs to rest more than she is. The town wants her to stay in the job. Like I said, I wanted to help. I didn't realize how much work this benefit involved."

She absorbed what I said. "My dad was sick too. Different disease, but it took his life. I understand how an illness can affect a family."

"I'm sorry." So, that explained the awkward family vibes. I backed out of the drive and turned the opposite direction we'd driven in.

"What you're saying is, I took the tree meant for the charity event."

"Yes."

She pressed a hand to her forehead. "Yikes."

"I could have taken your tree and left your car in the ditch," I added. "Turns out, I'm not Scrooge McGrinchy Satan-pants."

She pursed her lips. I wanted to grin again, but grinning would absolutely make her mad.

She turned in her seat to face me more fully. "You tried to convince me I bought too big a tree. The truth is, you planned poorly and didn't pick up your tree in time."

"Well—" She had me there. "Yeah, I did."

"Things happen to work out for you, don't they? Generally speaking."

I shrugged. "I suppose."

"You assumed without any planning or foresight, you'd put together a charity event in a couple days."

Heat crawled up my neck. "It's not that bad. I'm sure things will work out. Like you said." I flashed her my reliable Bennington charm.

A scowl hurled back at me. "That is so pretentious and privileged." She turned her head, looking out her window.

I wanted to argue our family wasn't part of some corrupt political machine, but I doubted she meant that. Her accusation stung. She wasn't wrong. I was used to not only getting my way, but having the time and freedom to figure things out. All but Mom's cancer, which I absolutely couldn't change. Now she and Dad needed me like they never had before.

And I'd been about to drop a bomb.

I'd planned on moving out of Crystal Cove. To finally start my own life.

Except...I couldn't leave them. No way could I move to my own apartment, look for my own job apart from the family printing business, right when our lives could change forever.

"I thought you were country-bred, but you're spoiled," she said.

I couldn't help laugh. "Country-bred? What's that?"

She gestured out the window. "Fields. Corn. Cows. Look, there's a barn."

"We have the internet out here, you know. Netflix. HBO Max. Stores, and culture, and art."

"Art?" She looked amused now. "What kind of art do you have in farm country?"

"There's a shop in town with a local artists' gallery. Paintings and sculptures. Our community center hosts a judged art show every year." The heat in my neck transferred to my face. "You know, for telling me I'm spoiled, you sound pretty stuck-up yourself."

She let out a single *ha*. "I pay my own rent, own my car, my own phone—all of it, without help."

"But you think anything beyond the city is trash. That's so...basic."

"I'm basic?" she blasted back. "I never said you were trash, to be clear. I grew up in the suburbs. I still have friends there."

"Do you visit them?"

She scoffed. "I don't need to explain myself to you. You're doing a lot of judging right now."

"Only because you judged me."

"You tried to manipulate me to steal my tree. Because you're a Fail Hard."

I gripped the wheel and hit the brakes. We slowly stopped with plenty of feet to go to the stop sign. *A fail hard.* She pegged me that quickly. Never left home, took the family job, but still didn't live up to even those lame standards.

We looked at each other, the tension thick as the ice coating the edges of the windshield.

"I wouldn't be driving you if I didn't feel a little bad about earlier," I admitted. "The...manipulation. I'm sorry."

"Fine." She sank back into the seat. "I didn't know the tree was meant for a charity event. I'd say sorry for buying it, but honestly the tree lot shouldn't have sold it."

"It's not your fault." I could only blame myself for assuming the Sawyers would keep the tree. And for assuming I'd plan the event in a handful of days. Here I was blaming a stranger for my own procrastination. A beautiful stranger, sitting so close, trusting me for some reason, to help her family holiday not suck with the perfect Christmas tree.

"You can have the tree—"

"Keep the tree—"

We stared at each other. A horn blared behind us. I hit the gas and headed past the stop sign through the intersection.

I cleared my throat. "Please, keep the tree. For your family. I'll get one myself for the mayor's benefit."

A few beats passed. "Okay. Thank you."

"You can help me load the new tree into the truck." I flashed a look her way to see how she'd react.

"Oh, will I?" Now her smile grew. "We'll see about that."

Chapter 5

Megan

When I agreed to this alternate holiday plan, I figured I'd spend time with Mom, ease into life with a step-family, maybe eat some glazed ham.

Not on my list?

Driving to a home improvement store in the sticks with a stranger. A cute but annoying stranger.

Nick Bennington wasn't a stranger to anyone else in this town.

Yet another familiar-to-Nick face stopped him in the parking lot on our way inside the big box store. Two others had already stopped us. "How is your mother?"

Nick smiled warmly. "She's doing well, thank you."

"I'm on the library board." The woman turned to a squiggling girl in pigtails whose hand she held. "This is my granddaughter Addison. Addie, this is the mayor's son. His name is Nick. Can you say hello?"

The girl ducked behind the folds of her grandmother's long wool coat. "Do you know Santa?"

Nick crouched to the girl's level. "As a matter of fact, I do. Our mayor's office receives a special telegram from Santa every year."

"What's a telegram?"

The grandmother laughed.

Nick grinned, and the little girl stared, captivated. "It's an old-timey way people used to communicate. Like sending text messages without a cell phone. Santa is coming in three days. Are you ready?"

"Yeah!" the girl squealed. She and her grandmother took off toward their car.

Well, color me captivated, too. "What, are you the holiday whisperer or something?" I mean seriously, who was this guy? He didn't even seem annoyed.

Nick paused at the automated doors, waiting for me to walk ahead of him. Once he caught up, he grabbed a cart. "I'm used to it. Before my mother became mayor, she sat on the city council and every committee you can name in this county. Our family owns a printing business that connects us to all the surrounding towns. Being out in public for me, this is how it is."

I zeroed in on the holiday decor at the front of the store. "I would hate so much attention. Having total strangers come up to me."

"I guess living in Chicago helps, huh?"

"I can grocery shop in peace and nobody needs to be told my life story a hundred times over."

"Must be nice."

I expected a snarky expression to pair with that statement, but Nick appeared thoughtful. Probably thinking I'm the nutbag who doesn't want to socialize when I'm out shopping for necessities like tree stands for a ten-freaking-foot tree. A tree more fit for a mayor's mansion than my stepdad's house. How was I supposed to know the tree was meant for charity? I'd made such a stink about it and now Nick told me to keep the tree. The ten-footer belonged to me now. For better or worse.

The holiday decor section lacked anything remotely useful. No tree stands, for starters. Beyond that, a rack of blinking stringed lights—who used blinking lights? No thanks. A snowman lawn ornament missing half its carrot nose tipped toward me in a desperate plea. "This place is so picked over."

Nick held up a crushed velvet stocking with the name Noah stitched on the cuff. "Well, Christmas *is* in three days."

Fair point. "You'd think the number two destination for the winter holidays would keep stock aside for stragglers. If they're still selling trees, why not tree stands?" I turned only to find my rant landed to empty space. Great—ditched.

A young guy wearing a store vest approached. "Miss, I believe I have a few tree stands left in the lot outside."

Standing beside him, Nick. "I got help."

"Oh. Thanks." I turned to the salesperson. "Thank you. We'll head out there."

So, maybe Nick had a helpful side. Which included kindness to children and nosy grandparents. That didn't mean he escaped the spoiled and privileged tags.

We reached the fenced-in area with potted holiday greens, wreaths and the remaining trees. Pickings were slim but at least there were pickings.

"How about this one?" Nick stood beside a rather nice, though short, tree. The bottom branches extended with a fluffier flair than the others. If you could call a tree fluffy.

"Sure. It's cute."

He squinted, sizing up the tree. "With a purse and a scarf, sure. It could be cute."

I scoffed, hiding a grin. I pulled out my phone to check messages, expecting to hear from Cam or Zahira, laying on the guilt for convincing them to switch shifts. Huh. No messages. I tapped one out to Cam to check up anyway.

"Are you going to help me, or what?"

I looked up. Nick shook his head with forced annoyance, staring at me.

"You lifted the ten-footer into your truck and you need me for this twig?"

He grinned. "I told you I'd make you help."

Make me. Hardly. *Gah*. Why did he get under my skin so easily? I marched over. "You have younger siblings, don't you?"

"A brother. Were you reading up on me?"

"I could tell by your pestering ways. I bet you teased him a lot."

"A fair amount."

"Besides, when would I have time to look you up? We met today."

"Just now. On your phone."

"I checked in with work. Now, what do you need my help for again? This tree is like half the size of the other one."

"I don't. I wanted your attention." He flashed a grin that maybe dazzled the ladies on the Illinois-to-Wisconsin border, but would not penetrate these hardened city boundaries.

"Nice. Try." Okay. Maybe my boundaries weren't so secure. I hid my face to cover my blush.

With that, I bent at the knees, grabbed hold of the tree from the middle, and lifted, tightening my abs and using my leg muscles. Groupon-acquired Cross-Fit for the win. Needles jabbed my face, but the walk to the truck would go quickly enough.

I glimpsed Nick, slack-jawed.

"You gonna pay for that?" he asked.

"That's on you, Mr. Mayor's Son," I called over my shoulder.

⋅♥⋅♥⋅♥⋅♥⋅♥⋅

"I hope you don't mind, I have another stop," Nick said once we were back in the truck, the new tree securely tied in the truck bed and the tree stand wrapped in a bag at my feet in the cab.

"Another stop? The mission was to get a tree stand. Tree stand and *your* tree acquired."

Nick turned out of the store lot. "It's on the way, in Crystal Cove town limits. Not far from your family's house."

"Stu's house," I corrected.

"Pardon my intrusion, but you're going to have to get used to the Stu thing."

"Pardon not accepted. My family isn't any of your business."

"Come on. Stu is a decent guy. My parents have known him for decades. His daughter made all-state track. She was two or three years ahead of me in school—"

"Good for her," I cut in. Stu's overachieving kids prickled my nerves. I wasn't proud of my irritation, but I couldn't help it. "Sorry. This is all new for me."

"All I'm saying is give him a chance."

Nick drove silent and steady until we reached a four-way stop. "I need to stop by this supplier to get the decorations."

I tapped my phone awake, but no messages waited for me. Fine, then. I slipped the phone back into my purse. "Don't you already have decorations?"

He let out a slow sigh. "Remember when I said I may have left some of the benefit planning to later? Well, the deal is you're supposed to pick a boutique to supply the decorations and they get the credit and free advertising. It's a whole thing. Obviously, my mom is great at it. She even gave me a list." He signaled toward a crumpled piece of paper in the cup holder.

I grabbed the paper and spread the page across my thigh to de-crinkle. The names of floral and home decor shops were listed one through five with handwritten notes in a delicate, loopy script. Clearly, his mother's handwriting. "So, which one are we going to?"

"I figured I'd start with the closest one on Barrington Road."

"Start with?" I held up the paper. "Let me guess. You never followed up with them." I looked at him, incredulous. "Any of them?"

A beat of silence told me everything.

"*Nick.*" I sounded far more exasperated than reasonably necessary given his emergency was not my problem. "It's three days until Christmas. What, are you going to just walk into one of these shops and ask them to professionally decorate a tree with three days' notice?"

"Actually, two days since Christmas Eve is the night of the benefit."

I swatted him with the paper. It made an unsatisfying *fwope* against his shoulder. "What if they all say no? What if they're already closed for the holiday?"

A horn honked behind us and Nick turned left. "They're all still open today. I'm not that much of a Fail Hard."

I wanted to believe him. He seemed like a decent guy, but it was like he expected life to fall in line around him. Life required effort. Work. Responsibility. Everything didn't simply *work out.*

I chose my words carefully. "The coffee shop where I work recently expanded to include event space. I've been the main contact to book musicians and private parties. So far, it's been a great boost for business. We've had to turn down a few requests because people called too late. We need adequate staffing for an event. If we don't have enough lead-time, it's too hard to cover with our limited staff."

"Makes sense." He turned again, onto Barrington Road. A small white building with a parking lot beside it and a sign for Vilmer's Floral came into view. Nick pulled in and parked. "I'll take you back after this. You don't have to come in. I'm sure you have people to message."

He opened the door and got out. The truck door shut again, the sound reverberating inside.

I flung open my door and followed.

Nick turned to me stomping toward him in the snowy lot. "What are you doing? This is my mess. I'll deal with it."

"With what, your Bennington charm?" I folded my arms and waited.

His chest rose and fell. "Yup." Only the yup wasn't the confident response he'd had earlier. Defeat deflated his whole demeanor.

"I'm coming with you." I breezed past him. "One thing I'm sure of. You need me right now."

Chapter 6

Nick

The bell chimed over the door at Vilmer's Floral. Inside, a pale woman with graying hair worked on an arrangement behind the front counter. She looked familiar but I couldn't place her name.

Didn't matter since Megan took charge. "Hello. My name is Megan. I'm here visiting my family for the holidays and your shop came recommended for a special request."

"How wonderful. Hello, I'm Nanette." She looked past Megan. "Nicolas Bennington?"

I cleared my throat. "Hey. Um, hello. Yes, I'm a Bennington." You'd think I could stick the landing on my own name.

"We'll be seeing you on the twenty-fourth for the benefit." She smiled, looking between Megan and me with an unreadable expression. "I can't wait to see who the mayor chose for the holiday decor this year."

Oh, man. This would be a rough one. Megan nailed it. The biggest Fail Hard in history title belonged to yours truly.

Suddenly, Megan slipped her arm through mine. I flinched and made a move to step back, but she shot me a look. *I know what I'm doing.*

"This has been *such* a hectic year," she said to Nanette. "With Mayor Bennington ill, we've realized just how much she does for the town."

Nanette's eyes softened. I never knew eyes getting soft was a thing, but her eyes had this squishy squint around them. She took us in— the me and Megan together thing—and nodded along.

Megan took in a measured breath. "I never would have believed we'd be in this place right now."

We? She squeezed my arm, hugging my body closer to hers. Honestly, I didn't mind. My heart flipped in my chest like some middle schooler seeing their crush in the lunch line. Except my crush held my arm. No, not my crush. A woman I happened to fail at convincing to give me her Christmas tree, who somehow ended up swindling for me. I'd owe her so big.

"We're planning a scaled-down benefit this year. Streamlined." Megan smoothed her hand across the counter for emphasis. "Really focusing on the charity instead of the pomp and circumstance, if you know what I mean." Her voice became gentle. "We want to be respectful of Mayor Bennington and not go overboard. I know it's terribly short notice, but we wondered if you had the time or desire to be part of our benefit. We're asking for decorations for one small tree."

Nanette stood in thought. "I'm so tickled you came here, but I'm afraid we're low on time. We wouldn't be able order what we need, or have the staff to put it together. Other than what we have currently in the shop."

No way would I interject anything at this point. I looked at Megan for the next move.

She stepped away from me and leaned her elbows against the counter. "Are all of your supplies spoken for? With orders? Would we be able to help put this together?"

"Let me take a look." Nanette opened a spiral book and moved to a desktop computer at the counter. "We had a failed delivery with no follow-up—some nice holiday greens with beautiful red accents we could donate as a table feature. We of course have holiday ribbon, some artificial berries, those types of things we could give to you."

"The table arrangement would be perfect. We'll be including all the businesses who donate in the printed program for the guests." Megan caught my eye and I gave her a thumbs up. Printed program —I could make that happen.

After ten more minutes, we walked out of Vilmer's with a huge holiday arrangement in a rustic looking planter. Nanette had given us a bag of ribbons and other stuff I had no idea what to do with.

"Boo-yah!" Megan pumped a fist in the air after the shop door closed behind us.

I stopped at my truck. "What was that back there? I mean, thank you, but...why are you helping me?"

She grinned ear to ear. This victory—a victory for me—boosted her into some sort of entrepreneurial master.

"Everyone seems to love your mom. I guess I feel bad she might not get the benefit she deserves. It was a worth a try."

Worth a try to help *me*. "I owe you a huge thanks." I set the arrangement in the truck bed, tucked in between the tree and a sandbag.

Back in the truck, I put the keys in the ignition. "I'm not sure I get the arm thing. You know, you putting your arm, like, being next to me all close." I mimed how she'd been touching me.

Her eyes danced with mischief. "Are you afraid I have cooties?"

"No," I blurted. Full blown idiot status achieved.

"I knew she'd only take me seriously if she thought I was your girlfriend."

"That's..."

"Sexist? Small-minded? More like a shortcut. She knew you by sight. It wasn't going to make sense to tell her the whole meeting-byaccident with the tree story. Besides, I never said we were dating. I implied it and let her fill in what she wanted." She beamed.

A flash of heat surged through me. I wouldn't mind having anybody think Megan and I were together. She used social engineering to get us a desired result. In college, I'd studied communications and business. I knew what this was. A means to an end.

I turned the key. "I'll get you home."

"What about the other shops?"

"What about them?"

"We only have one donation and some floral supplies. You're going to need these other shops to fill a whole mansion."

Heat spread into my fingers. "The mansion, it's not all that big. We all just call it that because it's the oldest house left in town and it used to be the largest. I'm only decorating the ballroom. Anyway, I'll figure it out."

"Nick. Think about your mom. What will make her happy? This party?"

It would. Taking a back seat in planning devastated her, especially in her final year as mayor. I'd promised her I'd make it special.

Now it seemed Megan cared whether I made it special. "Like I said. I should get you back." I turned onto the road. "You have better things to do."

She didn't say anything until a blinking yellow light met us at a crossroads. "My family is expecting me. You're right. I guess I got a little excited about the party planning part."

We pulled into Stu's long driveway. "Today probably wasn't what you expected. For me either."

She looked at me, like she expected me to say more. She tugged at a strand of hair, curling it around one finger. Something about that one move set my bones to jelly. She wasn't the hard shell she put out there. She saw a bonehead in need (that would be me) and cared to help. Unlike me, who preyed on a woman in the guise of helping. I didn't deserve her kindness.

Megan deserved to have a nice holiday with her family. Not to worry how I screwed up with mine.

I stared through the windshield, not willing to look back at her. To fully see how I'd tried to scam this obviously nice person. A beautiful, nice person who pretended for fifteen minutes to be my girlfriend.

"I wish you the best with planning. Sorry for all the mix-up about the tree." She opened the passenger door. "Thanks for the ride, Nick. I'll see you around."

If only I could be so lucky.

Chapter 7

Megan

"How was touring the town with the mayor's son?" Mom asked the second my boots came off.

Ah. The familiar sensation of immediate questioning upon entering the house. How had I forgotten? I held out the store bag. "Tree stand acquired."

Mom hugged me again. "I'm so glad you're here, honey. Once your brother gets in, everything will feel so right."

Okay, so I needed to let go of the crabby pants attitude. I smiled back. Feeling right sounded appealing. Derek had his work cut out for him.

Moving past the entryway, I stopped cold. "Whoa." The tree, laying on its side across the formal front living room, took up all the walking space in the room. Branches crushed against the edge of the couch. Two chairs were moved to the side and a coffee table into the hall.

No wonder the thing knocked me off the road.

"It's...big." Mom kept her voice light. "Maybe a touch smaller would have been plenty."

Stu strolled in. "Diane, it's perfect." He moved to Mom's side and gave her a sweet kiss on the cheek. "Glad to have you for the holiday, Megan. I imagine you're hungry."

Weirdly enough, I was starving and hadn't noticed. I typically lived on an eating-every-two-hours schedule. I was a girl who liked her snacks.

I handed him the tree stand and followed Mom to the kitchen, edging around the tree and keeping a bit of distance from the wild I'd brought into their home. Yikes.

Mom reheated a roasted vegetable casserole, which I ate with gusto. I missed this. My own cooking was a mix of take-out and recipes off Pinterest I used too many substitutions in to taste right.

After eating, Mom and I took on the task of decorating. Familiar boxes sat stacked on the living room floor now that the tree stood upright. Gentle piano music of a holiday classic drifted from speakers I couldn't see.

Mom slid a box with a bright pink lid toward me. "Look. Your childhood ornaments." A faded *Megan* written in permanent marker ran across the side.

I unclipped the plastic lid. A *Where's Waldo* figurine faced up with a Santa hat. Waldo's top lip showed an added black mustache.

Dad put that 'stache on Waldo. He'd said it would help his hiding tactics. I swallowed past the lump in my throat and gave Waldo a prime spot on the front of the tree.

We fished through the boxes, hanging every ornament. Our family legacy covered half the tree.

"Space them out, dear." Mom climbed the small three-step ladder Stu brought out and attempted to fill the top branches.

I stood back, taking in the view of the tree. What a weird tradition, decorating a live tree indoors with trinkets. Did anyone ever stop and think about this rationally?

Stu sipped coffee out of a Green Bay Packers mug. "Needs more lights."

"Maybe a few billion more."

He laughed. I laughed. Mom beamed at us.

"I bet we could find a good deal on some plain ornament bulbs." I rounded the tree, checking the branches facing the window. "Do you have a Target around here?" I could let Nick know if I found anything he could use for the mayor's house. Shoot. I didn't have his number. Maybe I could get the bulbs for him and—no. What was I thinking? Nick made it clear when he dropped me off he wasn't interested in, well, me.

Okay, maybe not clear. He hadn't been interested in driving to the rest of the shops on the list even though I'd offered. I stared at the portion of forest in Stu's front room. I'd taken Nick's charity tree. Of course he wanted to get away from me.

Mom wound a stray ribbon around her finger. "Stu and I were talking. We should look at buying you new tires. They're nearly bald."

My spine stiffened. "My car is fine."

"Honey, you're out there on your own. I worry."

"I told you I'd be okay and I am."

The ribbon uncoiled and she stuffed it in an empty ornament box. "Does the El train near you reach the university?"

"What?" Too late I realized my mistaking in asking.

"I was thinking—"

"Mom, don't—"

"Stu and I could help get you back on track with your classes—"

"I don't need—"

"So you can graduate."

And there it was. My failure stated out loud, ready to ruin Christmas one more way.

I collected my thoughts. Well, one of them, at least. "I don't need anything. *Anything.*" My sharp tone sliced the air like an ice pick.

Great start at a happy holiday, Megan.

·♥·♥·♥·♥·♥·

Nick

Christmas had to be the worst holiday ever. Too bad, because I used to like it back when I didn't have to decorate a mansion.

"Are you coming today?" my buddy Austin asked over the Bluetooth in my truck. "We're heading out with the snowmobiles at eleven."

I winced, glancing at the clock on the dash. I'd risen bright and early hitting the rest of the shops on my list. The shops I should have contacted weeks ago but the list got lost in the shuffle. Mom never seemed to have an issue running the town and planning a holiday party. She had plenty to shuffle.

"You still have that mayor thing going for your mom?" Austin asked as I parked behind the mayor's mansion.

"Yup. Tomorrow night. You're coming, right?"

"I guess I could come. See what kind of party planner you are."

"Not a good one."

He laughed. "I could've told you that."

For some reason, it stung. "Gotta go. I'll text you when I'm on my way."

I looked over the list again, shuddering at the memory of my encounters. The home decorating place listed as number two laughed in my face. Number three gave me a polite decline and wished me well. Number four, another florist with a gift shop, offered a discount on some holiday wares. Short on time, I took them up on it and left with strands of lights, a skinny wooden Santa thing, and some tinsel.

I was screwed.

I entered the mansion through the side entrance near the kitchen. Jill, who worked for the city and mayor's office, rushed toward me.

"Nick. We've been looking for you. I didn't want to bother your mother."

"I'm glad you didn't. What do you need?"

Jill had flushed peach skin and sprayed-up blond hair that both made her look younger and older. She had on a gold sweater with snowflakes knit into it. "I know we're doing things differently this year, but when will the decorating team arrive? I'd like to update my schedule."

She was looking at the decorating team. "I have a few things here." I showed her the bag. The tree I bought yesterday was already set up in the ballroom with white lights. No ornaments. "We're going for a scaled-back theme this year." I parroted what Megan told the florist at Vilmer's and hoped for the best.

"Hmm." Jill squinted at the tree before taking the bag. She scuffled through it then looked back at me. Her smile was the kind teachers gave to little kids. The one people too polite to say what they really thought gave to cover what they wouldn't say out loud. "Nick. You've been a great support to your family. How about I take it from here?"

Jill had me pegged. No theme, no team. Only today and half the day tomorrow to get this shindig rolling, and our wheels were frozen to the ground.

I couldn't give up this easily. "What can I do? I'm good at fetching. If you give me a list, I'll do the work."

Jill gave me her best Kindergarten Teacher. "I'm sure you will. I'll be right back."

I hit Austin's contact info in my phone. If the guys could hold off a few hours, I could join them. Or meet up later.

My phone buzzed in my hand. "Hey, Mom. What's up?"

"Just checking in. Did Jill talk to you?"

She knew. She knew I'd failed my one promise to her. I sighed. "I'm playing gofer to pick up whatever she needs." Which was what I should have been doing in the first place if I hadn't promised Mom the moon wrapped as a charity benefit.

"Good. She's a pro. I wish I could do more."

"Mom, no. Rest up. All you need to do is show up tomorrow. That's it."

"You're too good to me, Nicolas. I couldn't have asked for a more reliable, wonderful son."

I laughed. "Those meds are something else."

"Oh, stop, I'm serious. You've always been there for the family. It means a lot. I want you to know I'm thankful. I'm not sure what I'd do without you here."

I turned my back to Jill, though she'd wandered to another room. My throat jammed up. "I'm thankful, too."

She ended the call. I looked out the window across the sloping front lawn. The courthouse, the town square park and shops all in view. The bank marked the end of downtown, where the road returned to two lanes and pointed toward another town six miles out. The whole town in one glance. My own life plotted on the familiar points of the map. Same as always.

How was I supposed to leave? This town or my parents? Crystal Cove was home. I should be happy here. I hadn't ever wanted to leave before. Coming back after college—a choice I made myself. I hadn't gone far to begin with. But now...

Now, I'd lived here a few years on my own. The town and all its opportunities shrank to a grid I'd memorized and replayed daily. I couldn't go anywhere without a conversation about my family.

"Nick?" Jill handed me a list. "Crystal Gifts in town is expecting you. They have decor we'll use for the tree. They'll bring floral arrangements this afternoon."

I took the homework gladly. No room to feel sorry for myself since the clock counted down. I needed to finish this job and not run off while Jill fixed my mess. My day went from snowmobile to no-mobile.

The snow had stopped falling yesterday, but the cold air guaranteed the white stuff would stick around. I grabbed a knit hat and gloves from my truck. The driveway angled from the mansion onto Main Street, making for an easy walk.

A huddle of middle school-aged girls sipped warm drinks with white plastic lids outside Main Street Sweets. Mariah Carey's voice bounced between the shops and cars announcing what she wanted for Christmas. That song always got stuck in my head.

I entered Crystal Gifts headed straight to the sales counter. Or tried to. The place was packed. Shoppers bundled in winter gear stood in every aisle and crowded around glass displays. This was the kind of store a guy like me had to watch out in or I'd knock an expensive vase into an even more expensive vase.

"These are perfect, Mom. Look."

The voice caught me by the collar. I looked over my shoulder. Hoping, I had to admit.

Dark curls spilled from a familiar hat with a puff ball. Megan.

"Are there enough?" a woman asked, her back turned toward me.

Just then, Megan looked up and our eyes met. Her face brightened, then fell and ended up somewhere in the middle. "Hi, Nick."

The woman beside her swung around. "Nick Bennington. So good to see you again." Her voice carried, causing several people to gawk.

"Good to see you too, Mrs..." Had she taken Stu's last name? Didn't want to assume.

"Mrs. Krueger," she filled in. "But call me Diane."

Megan gave her mom a strange look, but quickly ditched it to smile tentatively at me. "How is the decorating going?"

"Oh, uh, good." I ripped my hat off, feeling hot all the sudden. "Jill from the mayor's office is handling things. I'm playing fetch." I waved Jill's list in front of me. "I got rescued is what I'm saying. So, problem solved."

"Oh." Megan's eyebrows furrowed. "Well, that's good, I suppose." She held a clear plastic box of round silver ball ornaments. "We're looking for more ornaments. Fifty percent off."

"You have a lot of tree to fill."

Megan's cheeks colored. I couldn't help but grin. She knew that tree was too big for the house. She knew but her pride—or something else—kept her from admitting it.

"Stu got the tree upright, so that's a small victory." Diane turned to her daughter. "Let me take these to the register. The line is getting long."

Which left me with Megan. Not exactly alone, but I didn't care to check on anybody else. "Thanks again for—"

"You gave up?" She closed the gap between us, her voice hushed and accusatory.

"What do you mean?" I stepped back from her advance, a stupid move that pushed my back against a display where glass trinkets tittered and clinked. I jerked forward, joining her space. She smelled like vanilla and Christmas.

"Let me see this list." She snatched the paper from my hand and scanned it. "Why is this Jill person giving you chores?"

"This *Jill person* has twenty years' experience."

Megan scowled, turning her brow down in a way that only made her more appealing to me. "Seems like with all that experience the benefit would be planned by now."

"She didn't step in earlier because I insisted on planning the mayor's part myself." And look what happened.

"My mom pointed out the mayor's mansion. It looks beautiful."

You look beautiful. I almost said it. Out loud. From my own dumb mouth. "The outside is great."

"And inside?"

Her question came out soft, curious. I was curious too. I wanted to see what Megan was like away from Crystal Cove. If we'd met some other way, not arguing about Christmas trees and my bad planning skills, things might be different.

"Nick?"

I blinked. "Yeah?"

"You look like you're having heat stroke. Maybe step outside for a sec."

I rubbed the back of my neck where sweat decided to hold a recruitment rally. I peeled off my coat, sending my elbow into the glass case behind me. "Crap."

Megan stretched past me and stopped an angel figurine from skydiving to her death. "I think you're giving up too soon. Look, here." She chose another box of the silver ornaments and shoved it into my hands. "A few of these with white lights on the tree? So pretty. Understated."

"I tried the scaled-back line on Jill. She didn't buy it."

Skeptical Megan was skeptical. "Jill isn't the mayor's son."

I laughed out loud at that one. "No, I suppose she's not."

The song overhead switched to a classic tune and I found myself humming along.

"Ha!" Megan clapped once and pointed at me. "You *do* like Christmas."

"Because I'm humming? I'm only human."

"Are you, though? I sensed you were The Holiday Whisperer. Prove me wrong."

"Even if I could whisper the holidays"—what did that even mean?—"my party planning days are over."

Megan seemed to chew over my comment when her mom returned.

"Honey, I just remembered I want to stop by the bank and the dry cleaners. Should I meet you back here in an hour?"

"Meet me, why? I'll go with you."

Diane gave me a sidelong glance. Ah. Diane Krueger, Matchmaker.

Megan realized it the same second. *"Mom."*

"I'm sure you'd rather spend time with someone your age after hanging out with Stu and me last night. Go on for now. Enjoy your day."

I carefully moved my gaze to Megan. Her eyes shone bright, cheeks pink enough to match her lip gloss. "I could use help bringing the decorations to the mansion."

We both knew that wasn't true. I didn't care.

"Visiting the mayor's mansion," Diane repeated. "That sounds fun."

Megan visibly took a breath. Looking at her mom and translating whatever she was reading on her expression, Megan smiled back at me. "Sure. That sounds nice."

I'd take nice if it meant spending time with her again. As much as I didn't deserve it, no way would I walk away.

Chapter 8

Megan

T he gift shop line now stretched halfway through the store.

Nick looked at me. "Let's give the staff a chance for the crowds to ease up before I bug them about the supplies. Interested in coffee?"

When wasn't I?

Nick and I ended up at Main Street Sweets two doors down. Adorable gingerbread creations danced in the window and glittering paper snowflakes twirled from strings. Inside, the scent of pure sugar mixed with rich coffee roast sent comforting vibes through me. Beside me, Nick's solid presence and his festive plaid scarf added another layer of vibes.

He caught me looking at him and my cheeks heated. I made a show of peeling off my coat now that we were inside. "Warm. In here. It's...warm."

Nick only grinned.

I ordered a flat white, my current favorite drink, curious how the shop would handle the balance of espresso and steamed milk.

"I'll have a coffee, black," Nick added over my shoulder while swiftly handing over a plastic card.

"Hey. I can get my own drink." Getting coffee didn't mean this classified as a date. No matter what my mom thought.

"Not in my town."

I rolled my eyes. "Here we go again with the Nick Bennington Display of Ego."

"It's egotistical to buy someone their coffee drink?" He pretended to look offended. "For someone who works at a cafe, I figured your order would have twelve parts."

"Sometimes simple is best," I offered, and sauntered over to the baked treats section. I picked out a bear claw with flaking pastry, and several cookies. After paying, I found a table by the window. I unwrapped my bear claw and bit into it. My eyelids involuntarily closed. *So. Good.* Amazingly good.

Nick found the table and sat across from me, setting down the drinks. I slid two cookies from the bag, a macaron and a shortbread, placing them on a napkin in the middle of the table.

"Ooh, these are awesome." Nick stuffed the macaron into his mouth.

"Macarons are more of a cookie you bite into." I stared as he munched the whole thing.

Now he was nodding with an expression that appeared to be deep contemplation about what he was tasting. He took a swig of coffee. "Man, is that good. Coffee and a cookie. Can't beat it."

The strangest, warm sensation floated over me. I couldn't nail it. Maybe the holiday spirit finally catching on? I attempted to simultaneously shrug the feeling aside and settle into it. "So, I was thinking. You still have ways you can make the benefit special. I know what it's like to want to do right by your family. When you have something to make up for."

"Like buying a mammoth Christmas tree? And by mammoth, I mean it's the size tree a woolly mammoth would choose."

I glared at him. Or, at least, tried. Maintaining a good glare while eating a delicious bear claw with sugar-coated pop music overhead proved challenging.

He sat back, taking another drink. I preferred to let mine cool off. I brought the flat white to my lips. Not bad.

"Good?"

"It's good."

"So, the City Girl is impressed by something the country made."

"Hey, I said the mayor's mansion was beautiful."

"I'll give you that."

"I couldn't ever live here, but it's nice to visit." I let my gaze wander to the window and the street buzzing with shoppers. This was the type of town you escaped to for the weekend, if you had the kind of job or money offering a chance to escape. For me, I worked weekends. I served the regulars looking to relax from their own jobs.

"Do you like it? Living in the city?"

"I love it," I answered immediately.

"What do you love so much?"

I ran my finger over the smooth, warm cup. "Everything I could want is nearby. All the good bands come through Chicago. Theater shows, art galleries."

"Us cow-hards don't know nothin' about no art."

I snorted. "Cow-hard? What is that?"

"I guess it's a cross between a Fail Hard and...a cow."

Call me a sucker but his dopey comment and genuine grin gave him an infectious charisma I couldn't ignore.

"So, you go to a lot of gallery shows?" he asked. "Concerts?"

I loved both, but I hadn't done much beyond work the past year. I'd been focused on getting my own apartment. No more roommates, a personal goal of mine. Working up to store manager was my next goal, which required taking on extra shifts and responsibilities. Work that would eventually pay off. "Sometimes. I work a lot."

"And you like your job?"

A question with an easy answer. "I do. I love it."

"What do you love about the cafe? What's it called?"

"It's called Drip."

"Drip. That is so *city*."

I laughed. "Yeah, I suppose so. But look, we're at Main Street Sweets. On Main Street. That's about as on-brand small town as it gets."

"Sometimes simple is best."

He had me there. "I'm good at making the drinks and it feels different a lot of days, depending what we have going on. We rent out our space for parties and book live music on weekends."

"That sounds fun. Stuff shuts down pretty early out here, except for Checkers and that's outside of Crystal Cove proper. You can't buy alcohol here after six p.m."

"*No.*" I slammed my hand against the table, causing an older man with glasses on a chain to frown my way. "Oops. Sorry, that was...I mean, I'm not much of a drinker to care." I was embarrassing myself.

Nick was looking at me with this weirdly rosy glow in his cheeks.

"What?"

He shook his head. "Nothing. You're funny."

"I wasn't trying to... Anyway. Hey, let's see if the gift shop has your stuff. Then you can tell me all about your awesome job and living in Small Town, Corner of Illinois, USA."

Outside, Main Street wasn't any less busy, but the gift shop no longer had a line. Nick handled his business, and the store staff led us into the back room. Two large boxes held tasteful silver and red decor. Ornaments, boughs of greens, ribbons and little decorative wreaths. Simple, standard decorations.

Nick slid the two boxes close to the back door. "It's a good thing you're here or this would have taken two trips."

"You think I'm carrying one of those?"

For a moment, Nick's expression flickered. Gone was the joker teasing about cows, replaced by a heavier mood.

"I'm kidding." I lifted the box. "I'll carry one."

"If it's too much, I can come back. You don't really have to help me."

"I'm already holding the box. I'm here to help."

He opened the door, held it open with his foot, and grabbed the second box. "Your mom sort of orchestrated this. Don't feel obligated."

I had stolen the charity tree. Stolen by paying for it, but still. "Just so you know, I do Pilates. I'm lean underneath these layers."

Nick's cheeks tinged rosy again and I grinned. So, flirty comments got to him. Check and check.

Chapter 9

Nick

We trudged uphill toward the mayor's mansion, Megan and I each carrying a box of decorations. Megan had to be regretting her offer to help me by now. I should have enlisted Austin and my buddies for the grunt work.

She seemed to barely break a sweat. "So, what do you like about your job? It's your family's printing company, right?"

"Yeah." I let her walk ahead. "How about you tell me more about living in Chicago."

"Um, sure. Never cross the street in front of a bus because they will run you down. It's annoying running errands downtown because of tourists. They stand in the middle of the street and gawk at everything." She slowed, shifted the box in her arms, and kept going. "Pro-tip: if you want to take in a city view or look up at some cool buildings, step to the side of the sidewalk first."

"The More You Know. Roger that—no gawking unless you pull over."

"For real, though. What's your job like? Can you make your own hours since it's your family's business?"

The box I carried grew heavier with each step. "Sort of. I mean, I'm here doing this instead of at the shop."

"Do you design anything? I guess I don't know much about what a print shop does."

"We do a lot of commercial orders. We aren't into the design part, but we can help customers choose the best format for their print jobs. I'm more interested in making our business efficient. Modernizing. Looking at greener options that reduce waste. This has to be boring for you."

"I asked. I'm curious. That's great that you can see your family business in a new light."

Except nothing about working for the family business felt new at all. Talking to Megan about my life in Crystal Cove reminded me of talking with classmates who'd left for good after high school. Their Instagrams showed them in cool places like Portland or Denver or Miami. Jobs as sports team trainers, web developers, a doctor in residency. Then me, a graduate with a business degree from UW-Madison, and I came right back home to get handed a job at the family company. My life was Crystal Cove, and the entire town limits could be seen from the top of this hill.

Finally, we reached the mansion's front porch. I set my box on the worn step and slid open the door.

Warm air shot through and the retro *Rockin' Around the Christmas Tree* blasted from a portable stereo on the staircase facing the entry.

When little kids saw a mall Santa or a pile of presents with their name on it, that was Megan's face right now. "Wow, it's gorgeous in here. Cozy for a mansion."

"I thought you didn't like Christmas?"

She tried glaring at me, but the bite never showed. She looked cuter than ever.

Jill had gotten to work arranging greens along the polished wood staircase banister, with some winter-looking flowers displayed in vases on tables. A rolled-up red carpet stood on its end by the door.

"Incoming." Megan tapped her phone. "My mom is asking my ETA. I'm going to tell her it will be awhile. She can get me on her way to the airport to pick up my brother."

"What? Why?"

"Because I'm going to help you."

The room shrank as her words hit. Accepting her help didn't feel right. "It's only these two boxes. I'll be fine."

Instead of answering, she texted with fast fingers. "Done. She'll check in with me on her way out." She smiled brightly.

"I like you being here," I paused, not sure I should have said as much. "But not if it means stealing your time away from your family."

She gave me a look translating to, *Wrong again, dummy.* "You said it yourself, my mom is the one who pushed us into hanging out. Besides, I spent plenty of time at House of Stu last night."

"You mean your mom's house. The Krueger house."

She flinched. "Sure. My small-town hideaway whenever I need an escape."

Funny that anyone saw Crystal Cove as an escape. This town held me in. Held me back.

"Okay. Give me the tour." She gestured to the surrounding room.

"You want a tour?"

"Of the mayor's mansion by the mayor's son? How could I refuse?"

"You can't usually refuse something that isn't offered." It sounded meaner than I meant. She bit her lip. Oh man, now I *couldn't* refuse. "I'll show you around."

I made for a sucky tour guide, but Megan didn't seem to mind. I answered her questions the best I could. When was the mansion built —1899. Kept in the same family for generations until they donated to the city and the house was designated a historic site. I'd never actually lived in the mansion, and as far as mansions went, this place wasn't all that big.

"Is this chair original to the house?" Megan pointed to a high-backed wooden chair with a nearly threadbare cushion.

Was it me, or were these questions getting harder? "Sorry. Jill might know." We finished upstairs and headed back down. "Would you believe me if I told you the house is haunted?"

Her eyes widened. "It is?"

"No. Sorry, it's just an old house." I handed her the brochure available to tourists. "You'll probably find this more helpful."

"You don't have to pretend there are ghosts here to make it sound interesting. I like learning about Crystal Cove." She blinked, almost like she was surprised to admit this. "I like hearing your version, at least."

Maybe I was overthinking the whole city versus country thing. I just needed to be me.

She pointed to a modern folding chair by the front door. "Can I sit for a minute?"

I nodded and she sat and opened the brochure.

"Hey, I'm going to check in with the folks." I took out my phone. "Be right back."

Mom's voice mail kicked in. I left a message saying everything was in order so far. I didn't want her worrying. I flipped through a couple of messages from my dad with an update about a print order. Another text from Austin. Knowing Megan waited in the other room made up for missing snowmobiling.

When I returned, Jill and Megan sat beside each other chatting.

"Jill, this is Megan. A...friend of mine." I hadn't introduced her to anyone yet. Friend didn't quite sit right, but that was probably me with my head stuck in the clouds.

"Wonderful meeting you," Jill said to Megan. She stood and handed me a sheet of paper. "I have more things for you to pick up."

Megan plucked it from my hand. "I'll take that."

Jill raised a brow, but said nothing and walked off.

"Hey, I can handle this."

Megan skimmed the paper and handed it back. "Do this stuff later. You have your truck?"

I was suspicious. Very suspicious. "Why?"

"Do you trust me?"

"Absolutely not."

She scowled. So cute.

"Put on the puff ball hat and I'll take you seriously."

She punched my arm. "I'm telling you to trust me. Will you trust me?"

"Are you going to tell me where we're going?" At this point, I'd made up my mind. I was going, even if I didn't know where.

She marched ahead, out the front door and into the brisk afternoon air. "Back where it all started. The Sawyer tree lot."

· ♥ · ♥ · ♥ · ♥ · ♥ ·

I had to admit, Megan's plan to return to the tree lot made me more curious than suspicious.

"The big trees are gone," I reminded her as we drove out of town toward the highway. "Remember, you took the last good one."

She stuck her tongue out at me.

"Mature." But I laughed anyway.

Only one car sat in the parking area. There were still trees left. We both jumped out of the truck.

Rob Sawyer waved, tugging an earbud free. He snapped his fingers and pointed at Megan. "Hey, I know you. How did you do with that giant tree?"

"It shook loose and then I slid off the road."

Rob's eyes nearly fell out. "What? No way."

Ethan stomped over in his heavy boots. "I told you. You never should have sold her that big a tree. I'm sorry, miss."

Rob looked past Megan to me. "Hey, Nick. We'll get to you in a sec." He turned to his brother. "I swear, I tied it really good. You aren't going to sue us, are you?" he asked Megan.

Ethan jabbed Rob. "You don't ask a customer that, dingus."

"Sorry. I obviously can't go back in time for a do-over."

"Actually, you can," Megan said. "Not the back in time part, but the do-over part. Sell us the rest of your trees."

"The rest?" Rob turned to the lot. "We've got like, twenty left. What are you going to do with twenty Christmas trees?"

I joined the group. "Um, Megan? What are we going to do with twenty trees?"

Rob's nose scrunched. "You're with her?"

No use in lying. Both Sawyers would know I'd been holding out if I'd never mentioned Megan working for us. Sharp, captivating, and obviously not a townie like us, they'd have made it their business to get to know her. "We met...later that day."

Ethan's eyes widened. "You followed her?"

I cut him a hard look. "I *found* her in the ditch with the tree she bought from you guys pointed into a bush."

Megan turned to me. "Did you find me? Or did you have a hot tip from these guys?"

Uh-oh. Fire smoldered in her eyes. I may have come clean how I'd tried to swindle her out of the tree, but she didn't know I'd sought her out.

She shot me a quick look and turned back to the Sawyer brothers. "If it's true you did a crap tie-job and you told Nick about it with some kind of hope he could take my tree, well, that makes this deal even more crucial."

Rob tugged at the cord of his ever-present earbuds. "I didn't tell him to go after you, I swear."

Every muscle in my body clenched. *Shut up, dude.*

"Shut up, Rob," Ethan said. "And what deal?"

Megan straightened, seeming to rise a few inches. "The deal you're giving us for these trees. You're going to deliver them to the mayor's mansion and place them along the driveway leading up to the house. We'll need white lights and extension cords. And an external power source."

Rob and Ethan looked at each other and burst out laughing.

"Megan," I said half under my breath. "I don't think—"

"You mentioned you didn't want me to sue you," she said, plowing straight ahead. "I know you were joking, but you should consider the legal ramifications. I filed an insurance report on my car after the damage caused by the tree. My attorney in Chicago is familiar with how these mom-and-pop joints work. They'll clean you out."

Ethan's jaw hung open. He looked at me. "Nick, what's this girl up to?"

I was stumped at the moment. "The Sawyers are family friends," I told Megan. "We don't need to threaten them."

"Then the decision should be easy. The benefit has a budget to cover what the Sawyers will take for the remaining trees."

"How do you know about our budget?"

"I asked Jill."

"I was gone for two minutes!"

She gave me a self-satisfied smirk. "I work fast."

Lost for words. That was me. Words with no sense of direction.

She turned back to the Sawyers. "Don't you want to close shop? Liquidate your stock, call it a day, and hang out at Checkers? It's the night before a big holiday. The place will be crawling with college students home for the holidays."

Oh, she was good. Ethan had the math going in his head. Rob already abandoned the math and jammed to his own soundtrack.

"Give her the deal, dude," Rob told him over the music in his headphones.

Ethan stroked his beard. "What are we talking here?"

"Well, the benefit is under budget because...reasons." She glanced at me, sparing further judgment how I had under-spent because I'd under-planned. "I see you have a generator and lights strung around your shack."

Ethan folded his arms. "It's an outpost."

One wood-slatted wall sat beneath a heavy-duty tent over top. Two sad wreaths hung askew on the wood part.

She held up a hand. "Sorry. Since we're taking all the trees off your hands, you'll give us a bulk rate. There should be room in the budget to buy more string lights. We need this all set up by two p.m. tomorrow. Deal?"

Ethan looked at me. "You're asking us to do the set-up?"

"I'm not asking you to do anything," I answered. "But if you're smart, you'll listen to Megan."

"You're getting the night off early to go to Checkers. Or don't go out and have the trees all set up tonight. Your call."

Ethan laughed despite himself. "Nick, you're cool with this? I mean, is she working for you now?"

"You gave away my tree." I threw up my hands. "This is the best solution I can think of."

"We're paying you for your inventory," Megan reminded him. "The manual labor is a bonus to make right the damage to my car. I'm sure the Sawyer family would appreciate a full-page ad in the program how you supplied all the indoor and outdoor Christmas trees." She turned to me again. "I was thinking we should bring a couple more into the house. Like that skinny one over there could work in the dining room by the built-in china cabinet, and that scrubby one? It has personality. That could go at the top of the staircase looking over the guests. Tinsel and a tree topper would be cute, like this one in the brochure." She showed me page three with the photo caption: *A Mid-century 1950s Christmas.*

A call back to historic decor at the mansion. "Dang, you're good."

She looked at Ethan. "Deal?"

He held out his hand for a shake. "Deal."

Rob guided Megan farther into the lot to inventory the trees.

Ethan clapped a hand on my shoulder. "I don't know what you got yourself into, but hang on to her."

Chapter 10

Megan

Nick said his goodbyes after paying for the trees and taking a written agreement about the set up. I'd insisted on the documentation.

I swung myself back into the passenger side of Nick's increasingly-familiar truck.

He clicked his seatbelt in place. "That was great."

"Yeah?" And I felt great. I had to be riding some kind of high after bossing those Sawyer boys around. Okay, not bossing. Acting like a boss. For some reason being out of my usual circumstances made it easier to act more confident. I didn't know whether I'd ever have taken charge back at the cafe, even though decisive actions and deal-making was exactly what I needed to do to take over managing.

"Absolutely. Lining the driveway to the mansion along where the guests arrive—it's going to look great."

"And another tree by the side entrance with the accessibility ramp," I added. "Definitely one with lights there."

"Another good idea."

"Good. I'm glad." I resisted the urge to minimize my accomplishment. Despite the bogus lawyer threat, I offered the Sawyers a good deal. I helped Nick sort out his party planning issue. A good deed done on the trip I'd been dreading. "So, what happens at the event? Is there a band?"

Nick laughed as he turned out of the Sawyer lot. "I wish. More like carolers, a piano player, and usually someone playing a harp or something."

"What's planned this year?"

Nick blinked. "Uh..."

"Nick." I shut my eyes. "Please—"

"Hey, I'm trying to remember. The mayor's office booked someone, I just forget who. I think it's a brass quartet. Or maybe a trip—thrice—what's the word when it's three of them?"

"A three-piece?"

He rubbed his forehead.

The unease in my chest couldn't be ignored. Being responsible mattered to me. I remained skeptical. "Who is the emcee? Do you have the audio visual worked out?"

"Yes." His voice tightened. "Believe it or not, our town knows how to host an event. Even if I don't."

A chill zipped through the truck cab. "I just want it to be great for your mom. Like you said you wanted for her."

He stared straight ahead at the road. "Seems like you're avoiding your own family's problems to focus on mine."

The accusation hit me square in the gut. I pressed my lips together, holding back a retort.

Nick...was right. This event was a welcome distraction from thinking about a home that to me felt like a rental. Stu's presence confirmed the thing I knew but hated thinking about. Dad wasn't ever coming back. Worse? Now Dad was replaced.

The decorated sign for Crystal Cove came into view with a second sign beside it listing the mayor. The Bennington name right there, branded and official. It only made me more irritated.

If I needed to butt out of Nick's life, he should butt out of mine.

"You lied about how you found me," I said quietly. "You thought you struck gold when you found my car in the ditch. You only stopped to get the tree for yourself."

He let out a short breath. "I'm sorry. I know it looks bad. I swear, I would have stopped no matter what to see if I could help." A beat passed. "You're right that I wanted the tree. I told you that outright."

"You seem to think you can do whatever you want and get away with it." I tried to lighten my tone, but the bitter edge couldn't be missed. "It's like you have everyone in this town wrapped around your finger."

"I'm more than the mayor's son."

His usual confidence didn't come through. He said it like he wanted to convince himself.

I should have been spending time with my family, not arguing and feeling bad for this guy I barely knew. What had gotten into me? "You can drop me off back at the gift shop. My mom will swing by on her way to the airport."

Nick slowed with the traffic passing through the central blocks of Main Street. He turned on a side street and pulled over in a driveway marked Deliveries Only. The automatic locks unlocked.

I felt the acute need to apologize for inserting myself in his life. For my attitude. For assuming him to be the cliché he consistently demonstrated. The more time I spent with Nick, the more I avoided my family. Fixing his life didn't fix mine.

Since the second I stepped out of my car on that country road, he'd been trying to charm me. Now the charm fell away, leaving a figure unvarnished and stone-like. I had no idea what to make of Nick Bennington.

"Thanks for the help today." He wouldn't look at me.

"Nick."

A calm smile replaced the stone. "You've been nice enough to humor me. Tell your mom thanks for letting you hang out."

"I didn't need permission to hang out. I wanted to help you."

"And you did. The event won't be nearly as terrible now." His knuckles turned white as he gripped the wheel.

"You're not a Fail Hard. I'm sorry I said that."

His grip loosened. "Go spend time with your family, Megan. I've got it from here."

I tugged on my mittens and gathered my purse. There wasn't much left to say at this point. "Sorry, Nick. Thanks for the ride."

Chapter 11

Nick

"She thinks I'm the biggest waste of space." The truth hit hard even one pint in.

Austin nudged my beer closer. "Drink up, buddy. You'll forget about the city girl in no time."

Checkers grew fuller by the minute with familiar faces home for the holidays. The faces were getting younger, which weirded me out. I didn't buy that these kids were old enough to drink.

Austin elbowed me. "Look. That's Darrin's sister."

I blinked. I'd only drunk half a beer so my vision wasn't the problem. "Isn't she twelve?"

"Dude. She's at least a junior in college. University of Chicago, I think. Go say hi."

Chicago, like Megan. No thanks. I'd stick to townie girls with low expectations. Ugh. I rolled my eyes at myself. I was the one with low expectations. About myself.

Austin waved at the young woman. Black wavy hair, tawny skin, and definitely no longer a tween. She and her friend sauntered over, stretching their hellos into multiple syllables.

The conversation floated around me. I must have said enough to keep it going because Darrin's sister—Kelsey, was it?—and her friend kept on talking. And talking.

"Well, if it isn't Mr. Mayor," a loud voice boomed. Ethan Sawyer turned up at our table in a fresh checked flannel. "Nick, I don't know if I should thank you or slip into your house in the dead of night with a switchblade."

Austin slid his stool closer in. "What'd you do now, Bennington?"

"Sorry about earlier," I told Ethan. "The last few days have been something else."

"Where's Megan?" Ethan scanned the area, his gaze landing on Kelsey and her friend, where he flashed a grin.

"Picking up her brother from the airport."

I should have said I didn't know what Megan was doing. Her life wasn't my concern—she'd made sure of that. "There's nothing between us, if you're asking."

Ethan snorted. "Whatever. You've got it bad."

Kelsey leaned her elbows against the table. She looked at Ethan instead of me. "Tell me about this Megan."

"She's the reason I'm here tonight," he answered.

"What?" Every nerve flared. What did Ethan have planned with Megan?

Ethan caught the sleeve of a server walking by and ordered drinks for the table. He turned back. "And?" I pressed.

"She got Nick to buy out the inventory at the tree lot. We're closed for the season." Ethan lifted a water glass in a cheers with the rest of the table.

I knew that. I totally knew that.

"Way to go," Austin said, nodding his approval. "So, Nick. How about *you* tell us more about this Megan?"

He already knew my thoughts on Megan—at least what I shared when the two of us were talking. Thinking about Megan didn't mean I wanted to talk about her. Out loud. To the rest of the table.

Couldn't a guy hang out with his friends without the third-degree questioning?

Ethan waved me off. "Never mind, dude."

My shoulders eased. "Thanks. It's been a long day."

"I mean never mind because Megan can introduce herself. She just walked in."

·❤·❤·❤·❤·❤·

Megan

"Megan, over here!"

Whoever was calling my name had to mean another Megan. Calling out Megan in a bar was like asking for an Emma in a kindergarten class.

My brother, Derek, stopped walking and looked straight ahead. "I think that table knows you."

In the middle of the restaurant, I saw him. The one not shouting or waving. Nick. Beside him, Ethan from the tree lot, a guy I didn't know, and two college-aged girls who were probably hanging off the arms of Mr. Mayor's Son moments before.

I held up a tentative hand and waved back. I jacked Derek in the ribs. "I told you this was a bad idea."

Derek slipped his phone into his coat pocket. "Yelp says this place has good chicken wings. More importantly, it's open."

"We have food at the house."

"Mom wants us to live our young lives, bonding as only siblings can." He flashed a teasing smile. "Are you going to say hello to them or what?"

I whipped around, turning my back to the table. Who knew what Nick had told his friends about me since this afternoon. "It's a trap. We—me and Nick—didn't leave on good terms." I scoffed at my own statement. "I mean, there isn't a *me and Nick*. I met him yesterday and Mom forced us to buy a tree stand and have coffee together." And I continued to help him, but that was beside the point.

"I don't know about you, but I'm hungry. Looks like they have room at their table." He angled past me.

I watched, jaw open, as my brother completed his betrayal. Fists were bumped, table space cleared, and just like that, Derek was absorbed right into the group.

I gritted my teeth and walked over.

"We don't bite, I promise," the guy beside Nick said.

Nick abruptly stood, knocking his barstool into the person behind him. "Sorry." He scrambled to adjust the stool. "You can sit here. I mean, if you want."

His friend had a grin as wide as the Cheshire cat's. "Or you can have my seat and sit by Nick. I'm Austin, by the way."

Introductions flew and I found myself sitting in Austin's place as he circled around to Kelsey, the cutie in the UIC sweatshirt. I pointed to her shirt. "Hey, great school."

"Do you go there?"

"Uh, no. I live in Chicago, though."

"Oh, awesome. Are you alumni?"

I shook my head no, my grin frozen. Not even close. Community college for me, and I couldn't even finish that. I mean, I could have gone into debt for a generic humanities degree I didn't care about. Dad was fine with my slow-track degree plan. Stay at home, work, and take local classes. Then I had the zany idea to move to the city with a friend and take time off from school. Gain life experience. And once Dad was gone, going back to school never felt important.

"Megan lives in an amazing apartment in Chicago," Derek said, offering me cool points, which was possibly the nicest thing he'd said about me to other living humans. "It's above a bike shop."

"Like motorcycles?" Austin asked.

I shook my head. "Bicycles. A lot of people ride bikes in the city."

I thought I heard an appreciative "Oh" come from Nick, but couldn't be sure. Besides, I refused to look at him.

The server came by and a beer slid in front of me. Ethan pointed to the pint. "That's on me. Closed for the season." He raised his own glass in a salute.

Relief washed over. "I thought for sure you'd chew me out for that."

"Me? Naw." He waved me off. "I wish I'd thought to ask Nick to do this last year."

I took a sip. "Where's your brother?"

"The beauty of being older? I'm here. He's working."

I almost felt bad for Rob setting up all those trees by himself at the mansion. I glanced to Nick. Our eyes met and he quickly looked away.

Nick straightened in his seat. "So, um, Derek. Where do you live?"

"Seattle. And before you ask if I'm a Seahawks fan, yes, but I'm die-hard to the Bears above all."

The conversation flipped to football, where Kelsey made everyone jealous by sharing about her connection to a superfan who took her to a VIP party with the Chicago team.

Beside me, Nick fiddled with a paper straw wrapper, folding and unfolding. "I'm sorry how I treated you when we first met," he said low for just me to hear. "I shouldn't have lied."

Everything I'd seen from Nick spelled out considerate. He had asked more than once if I was hurt when he found me with my car in the ditch. He'd driven the tree to Stu's. He hadn't wanted to bother the gift shop staff when they were busy, even though they expected him. All that, and he still seemed down on himself.

A guy who skated by in life wouldn't have done those things.

"Did you get everything worked out for the benefit?"

He one-shoulder shrugged. "A few more loose ends turned up. I think I have it under control." He wadded the straw wrapper into a tiny ball. "You weren't wrong when you asked about the AV equipment and the emcee. Usually, the mayor makes all the announcements. My mom will be there, but we have another member of the office running the program this year. I made sure it's covered."

I ran my finger down the cool pint glass. "It wasn't my business to question you like that. I'm sorry."

Nick looked up. His jaw softened and his eyes shone with interest.

My heart did a backflip. So what if Nick had country boy good looks? I never fell for that. I didn't listen to country music. Like, ever. And I didn't like leaving the city. I looked away, desperate for a distraction.

"I love this song." Kelsey edged away from her stool and danced beside the table the way only a college student back in her hometown could.

Derek ate it up. Check that—every guy at the table gawked at Kelsey. I glanced to Nick only to find him watching me. I swallowed, my throat tight. I nodded toward Kelsey as she recruited more dancers from another table. "Your friend. She's cute."

"She's the younger sister of a guy I went to school with."

I nodded, unclear what I was meant to do with that information. "We keep running into each other. It's weird."

"Small towns do that."

"As long as it's not something mystical. Like holiday magic." I made my eyes go googly and fluttered my fingers around.

"Watch out." He signaled past me.

I followed his gaze. "What am I looking for?" Oh. Mistletoe. Threatening its menace from a wooden beam above the bar. "Ha. Right." As if I'd find myself underneath it. As if I'd be willing to accept the kiss toll the mistletoe required.

I turned back to Nick whose cheeks looked decidedly pinker.

Something tugged at me I couldn't ignore. "You seem...not so happy. I know a lot is happening with your family. Is that all?"

He sat slumped, his festive spirit sapped. Across the table Nick's friends laughed with the neighboring table. Even Derek gestured with his pint acting out some story. And Nick? Moping and apologizing.

Nick sat back. "It's loud in here. Want to step outside?"

"Sure."

Outside, the Checkers parking lot offered a glimpse of the glowing downtown Crystal Cove lights, like lanterns set at the edge of a dark room. In the other direction, the road disappeared into inky black. Our boots crunched over crisp, hardened snow.

"I want to leave Crystal Cove," Nick said.

My intake of breath hit sharp from the cold. I waited for him to say more.

"And my mom is sick. So you've heard." He rocked back on his heels. "I leave, and I'm a bad son. I don't leave, and I'm stuck here with my life mapped out."

"What would you do? If you left?"

He hung his head back, looking at the sky. "The stars are so bright here. I'd miss that in the city, right?"

"Where, Chicago?"

He nodded. "I look at advertising and marketing jobs every day. Then I did something stupid."

"What?"

"I applied for one."

"Let me guess. They called you back."

His gaze went back to the sky. "The literal day Mom got the diagnosis."

My heart tugged. "I'm sorry. What—" I almost asked *what did your mom say,* but of course he hadn't told her. "How long ago?"

"About six weeks. I still look at the job listings. I asked around with some friends I graduated with. I got a call last week from a distillery in Madison who wants a regional sales rep. The job would take me all over the Midwest."

"That sounds exciting. A chance to travel. What did you tell them?"

"I agreed to an interview."

He stated this with all the exuberance of a twice-annual dental cleaning. "Gee. You sound *thrilled*."

He rubbed at his beard scruff. "I guess it doesn't feel big enough. The guy even told me I wouldn't have to move. I could stay right here in Crystal Cove and pretend to go other places."

"Come on. You'd be traveling. I'm sure that part was true."

"And I'd come right back here. Same as always."

"To holiday splendor." I flashed jazz hands and did a little feet-in-place-but-I'm-supposed-to-be-dancing jig.

Nick laughed. Success.

I let my hands fall to my sides. "You know, there's a lot to be said about following your dreams. Whatever that means for you."

"Oh? What's to be said?" His eyes had a teasing light to them. He stood closer now, our coat sleeves touching.

"You never know until you do it." Open fields behind the restaurant mocked me. Living my best life-giving advice outside a townie bar in Crystal Cove? Who was I to give *anybody* advice? "I started with a dream. I guess I don't know what happened along the way." I ground my boot over the hard-packed snow. "I dropped out of college and moved to Chicago. My mom was furious."

"Why did you quit?"

"I didn't care. At all. I enrolled at community college near my house in the suburbs. It felt like high school all over again except without the fun parts—friends, basketball games, yearbook. The classes were basics to prep for going to another college I didn't care about."

"So, college wasn't the right fit."

"And Dad was fine with it. Dad…" I hated this part but it made more sense to say it. "He died the year I moved out. He hadn't been feeling great for a while, but he had a history of health problems. Nothing major, at least not that I thought. High cholesterol, high blood pressure, pre-diabetic. All stuff he worked on controlling with diet and medication and all that. My mom's a nurse—was a nurse. She retired early. She was always on him about appointments. I think sometimes he told her he went but didn't go." I covered my mouth, in shock the words fell out. "I shouldn't have said that. I love my Dad. I'm sure he… I mean, I don't have proof he didn't go to his check-ups."

Nick drew closer. "What happened?"

"Heart attack. As basic as it comes. Nothing fancy. A standard heart attack."

"Megan. I'm so sorry."

The hurt washed over me again. Not as intense as the first years, but still enough to remind me how much losing him wrecked me. Dad believed in my dream to live in the city and explore life. I didn't have career goals like my brother and every other ultra-achieving high school graduate in my class. My list of state school acceptances wasn't exactly impressive. Dad assured me that was okay. He'd rather I live my life the way I wanted, so long as I worked hard and took responsibility for my actions.

When Dad died, it was like that validation left with him. What remained were shortcomings and forgotten dreams. Explore life? I barely did anything except work and hang out after my shifts at the cafe with my coworkers or a few regulars. My bank account didn't leave many options for exploration. I shouldn't have left home. I should have stayed and made sure Dad attended his doctor appointments. At least I'd have finished a two-year degree. At least. At least that.

"Diseases don't have to be fancy to hurt or change our lives," Nick said softly. "Cancer is basic too."

"Nick. Ignore me, please. You and your family are going through so much with your mom right now and here I am whining about my dad who's been gone for four years."

"It's not a contest." He moved a strand of hair from my eyes. "No wonder it's hard to see your mom remarry."

"Right?" I appreciated the validation. "I could never say that to her."

"Maybe in different words. You could tell her what you're having trouble with. If she doesn't know."

"She wants me to go back to school. She even suggested it again last night when we were decorating the tree." I scrunched my face. "She and Stu would pay for it."

Nick clenched his jaw. His mouth twisted and he coughed. He was covering up...a laugh.

"What? What are you not saying?"

"Nothing. It's not appropriate."

The bar door opened. A large man in light-up deer antlers stumbled out. Another man steered him toward the passenger seat of a red car with plastic antlers attached to the roof.

"What were you saying about appropriate?" I asked.

"Okay, fine. You called me spoiled and you're complaining about your parents wanting to pay for college."

"Agree. That sounds textbook spoiled. But you don't have the full story. I need to prove myself. I need to show them I can make it without their help."

Nick scratched his chin. "Why again?"

"Because otherwise I did it for nothing. I moved away and left Dad for no reason." My confession burst free, permeating the air and hardening into ice. Solid and definitive, I couldn't take it back. I wanted to shatter it to pieces.

"Megan. You can't believe that."

I did. I believed exactly that.

"It's not fair to believe it," he went on. "If you don't want to finish college, that's one thing. But refusing help because you feel guilty for leaving home can't be good for you or your relationship with your parents."

"You keep saying parents plural. It's mom and Stu."

"Stu Krueger. Great guy."

Embers smoldered inside me. "I thought we came out here to talk about you."

Nick studied my face, setting me further on edge. "I didn't know you were hurting this much."

I was best at that. Not letting people know.

· ♥ · ♥ · ♥ · ♥ · ♥ ·

We made our way back inside Checkers. I stopped short a step past the door. I couldn't believe my eyes.

Half the restaurant had gotten to their feet, tables pushed aside to clear room for an impromptu dance floor. Okay, maybe not impromptu as a DJ jammed along to the song at a table shoved in the corner. Austin and Kelsey twirled in time to the music. My brother— *my brother* was dancing. Last time my brother danced in my presence he'd been wearing his high school graduation suit and fake breakdancing with his buddies.

"Want to dance?" Nick's voice sidled close to my ear. He stood right behind my shoulder.

I whipped around. He held a hand out. "You want to dance? Here?"

"It's Christmas."

His response made sense. Ridiculous and somehow perfect. Involuntarily, I looked up. No mistletoe. A pang of disappointment hit. No, not disappointment. Relief. Surely relief.

The song changed over to a familiar tune played at weddings and graduations. The dancers assembled themselves in rows and stepped in time to the song.

Suddenly, Nick's hand covered mine and I moved forward, pulled along by his strong grasp. Still in my puffy coat, we landed at the edge of the dance floor, shuffling right, left, then swaying and dipping.

Nick peeled off his coat and gestured for me to do the same. He dashed off to stash the coats at the table within the time it took to shuffle back. Seamlessly, he rejoined the dance, adding an extra dip and twist.

Color me impressed. "How'd you learn to do that?"

"I'll take that as a compliment." His boyish smile carried a shade of maturity. He *owned* this dance.

We stepped to the music, knocking elbows a few times (definitely my bad), growing nearer to each other with each step as more dancers filled in around us. This was like *Footloose* after the town broke the dance ban. *Everybody cut loose!*

He turned in the dance and caught my eye again. "What's your dream? You never said."

I hadn't said. Maybe because I didn't know.

One thing I did know—my dream wasn't to manage the cafe.

The next song took a turn for country, and the dancers stayed in their rows. They stepped to a new dance I'd never seen.

Nick grabbed my hand. "This one's fun. Watch."

He shuffled, did two quick steps, swiveled and turned—and I was lost. I tried to catch up and stumbled over my own feet. My boot's thick rubber sole caught the floor and sent me pitching forward into Nick's arms.

He caught me easily, like he'd been waiting for my blunder. "Whoa there. Are you okay?"

The room and the dancers fell away. Nick's eyes sparkled green. Like pine. Like Christmas.

"Uh-oh. Don't look up."

I knew before I looked. The crowd had nudged us closer to the bar and that pesky dangling plant with skinny leaves and white berries.

Still in his arms, I offered, "You know, mistletoe is a parasite. They steal a portion of their energy from other plants."

"Are you suggesting you want to steal my energy?" Nick's lip twitched.

I discovered I liked that lip twitch. I liked it quite a bit. "Maybe a nip of your holiday spirit." I leaned in before I could talk myself out of it.

Nick met me the rest of the way. His lips were softer than I expected. Warmer. Sweeter. Minty. I sighed into him and kissed him.

It wasn't a peck. It wasn't over quickly. I kissed Nick Bennington and I meant every moment of it.

Chapter 12

Megan

Kissing turned out to be way better than arguing.

I'd kissed Nick. And he'd kissed back.

All way back to Stu's I replayed our kiss. While I powered down for the night and settled into the guest room with a faded Miami floral vibe, I imagined kissing Nick somewhere besides a crowded townie bar. Under mistletoe, in tree lots, in the town square.

I liked Nick. A Christmas miracle.

Honestly, the things that bothered me about Nick were things I needed to face myself. He belonged somewhere and didn't appreciate what he had. Nick had an identity that people valued. He took that for granted. He wanted an escape, but didn't seem to want to work for it.

Whereas I'd escaped, working hard, but for what? What did I truly want?

I loved the cafe, but what I loved wasn't the managing part. I liked talking to the regulars. I liked connecting people to what else the city offered. I knew our little block of businesses and local services to recommend. What could I do with that?

Lying in bed, I pulled up Nick's number. We'd traded phone numbers at the bar, but I had the feeling I wouldn't need it. The second I left the house tomorrow, he'd turn up where I went.

Sleep not coming easily, I pressed my lips together, thinking over the kiss. How Nick tasted. How it felt with him holding me. I drifted off.

Morning came too soon by way of blistering sunlight through thin tropical print curtains. Stomping feet sounded outside the door. Pretty hard to stomp on carpet, but whoever thundered through the hall sure made themselves known.

I cracked open the door. Derek wore loose jeans and a faded War on Drugs T-shirt (the band, not the initiative) and lugged a box down from an attic ladder. "You've got stuff up here too."

"It's seven"—I tapped my off-brand fitness tracker until the time blinked on—"twelve in the morning. Don't you have jet lag?"

"I couldn't sleep. I got up at six-thirty and made coffee."

"Megan," Mom's voice destroyed any lingering hope of a gentle wake-up. "Derek will put your boxes in your room. It's mostly old teen magazines and school papers. Maybe a bike helmet."

I retreated to the guest room and shut the door. It was way too early for this.

My phone blinked on the bedside table. A text message from Nick waited for me.

Nick: Morning, Sunshine. Happy Christmas Eve.

I felt his arms and lips all over again. I typed back a response.

Me: You're up early on a holiday, Is that normal for this part of the state?

Nick: Standard. It's in the manual.

Me: I could use some of your holiday energy. Mom has us cleaning out our childhood.

Nick: Wow, the whole thing? Childhood covers a lot of ground.

Me: You're telling me.

Nick: All I've got is this mistletoe, see...

I chewed at the inside of my cheek, fighting back a smile.

Pounding sounded on the door. Only Derek pounded at doors like that.

"Just a minute. Gosh!" I was suddenly twelve again. I flung the door open. "You've been stomping. It's so loud."

Derek lumbered in and set a box in the middle of the room. The most inconvenient location possible. "I wake up at five fifteen every morning. Hit the gym and head to the office."

"You're so corporate."

He rolled his eyes. "Welcome to life with a real job."

The breath left my chest like I'd been punched. "I have a real job."

"You know what I mean."

I folded my arms. "No, I don't know."

He'd already backed out of the room, returning to the attic ladder. "I'm salaried. I have clients and benchmarks and company gainsharing."

I stepped over the box and out into the hall. "Sometimes I'm the only one to open or close the cafe. I book our entertainment and coordinate our rental space. All in addition to making drinks and serving customers."

Derek disappeared up the ladder. "Can you get this?"

He handed down a box labeled with my name. I shoved the box next to the other one in the Miami room. "You don't think I have a real job?"

He backed down the ladder. "I think you're intent to prove you do."

"So, it's not a career. So what?"

"Why are you so bothered by it?"

"I'm bothered by you. And Mom. And Stu. They want me to go back to college."

"So, go."

"I don't want to."

"Then don't?"

I grunted my frustration.

"You're smart. You could be doing more if you wanted. Dad—"

"Don't tell me what Dad would have wanted. Dad supported my move to Chicago."

Derek pinched the bridge of his nose. I guessed it was better than a shove, what he would have done as a kid. "*I* support your move to Chicago. I told your friends yesterday you had a cool apartment and I meant it. You're doing your thing."

He rubbed his eyes, the time difference starting to set in. "All I'm saying is you seem bothered by the comments, and if you're bothered, do something. You don't have to do what I do. Figure it out."

He acted so cavalier about it. Figure it out. Figure *life* out. Sure. Fine. Easy.

I went back to bed.

Chapter 13

Nick

I had to hand it to Megan, the mansion looked great. One hand for the Sawyer brothers for the physical work they put in lining the driveway with trees. A single red bow dripped from each treetop along the driveway. The last two trees flanking the end of the drive had the red bow and white lights. Worked for me.

All day, I followed Jill's lists, tying up loose ends, making calls, and giving instructions to volunteers. I couldn't say I enjoyed it, but pulling my weight with what I promised at least felt satisfying.

"Nicolas, this looks beautiful."

"Mom." I set the box of programs on a table covered in red plaid. "You're here early. You look nice."

She straightened the sleeve of her gold beaded jacket. "You did great."

"Jill did great."

"Don't underestimate yourself."

I couldn't take credit, but I didn't want to argue. "I have something to talk to you about." Here goes. "I've been looking for a new...opportunity."

She nodded. "I'm sure you hadn't envisioned working at the printers forever."

Just then, the sound of chattering young voices carried over. The kids' choir burst into the ballroom in a mob of sound and limbs. Mom immediately greeted the kids and the sponsor teachers. Any hope of a heart-to-heart needed to wait.

My friend had texted that the distillery could do a video interview the day after the holiday. Have me in Madison by the end of the week for a facility visit. I wanted to tell Mom. If I told her then I could tell Megan.

Megan and I had been texting all day.

Megan: Stu's kids are a trip. All-state in track, you said? How about all-state in all-everything.

Nick: But do they know about a flat white?

Megan: You remembered my drink! Most impressive.

Megan: Almost as impressive as a PhD in Electrical Engineering who researches particle physics and a doctor who spends vacations giving free treatments in impoverished countries.

Nick: Which is almost as impressive as making *a flat white.*

Megan: Ha-Ha. You're funny.

I didn't care how many degrees Stu's kids racked up. Megan doubted herself and I hated that. She didn't need a degree to make an impact. She'd already made an impact on me. And from the looks of it, on our benefit.

Nick: Please come tonight. You can be my guest.

I'd asked her last night before we left Checkers to come to the event. After we'd kissed. I couldn't believe she did it. She'd kissed me. For a second, I had to admit, I'd wished I'd made the first move. Then again, I'd steered us under the mistletoe. She'd taken the bait. I didn't mind being bait.

That kiss flipped a switch in me. I needed to show Megan I wasn't a simple townie riding my family's privilege.

Megan: Mom and Stu are pretty pumped about their holiday ham. We're doing gifts and games with the kids—that's Stu's grandkids.

Nick: A holiday ham, nice. We've got shrimp toast. We can't compete with a ham.

Megan: The ham is fifteen pounds. I've been hearing about it all day.

Nick: To match your fifteen-foot tree.

Megan: Hey. Only ten feet.

Megan: I can't believe it fits in the house.

I texted a gif from the Chevy Chase holiday movie where Clark and fam find the perfect tree in the woods complete with holy light shining from the sky.

She texted back an emoji smiley with the tongue sticking out.

Nick: No worries. Enjoy the time with your family.

The little dots danced on my phone screen, showing she was typing more. The message never came, and I was called off to another task.

Two hours later, the benefit had started, opening remarks were made, and the children's choir performed their third song. Guests strolled through the ballroom, eating appetizers and desserts while making bids on donated items for the silent auction. I made sure the photo booth line stayed manageable and assigned a volunteer to monitor the holiday-themed props.

My parents walked over with Jill. "How are you doing?" I asked Mom, taking her by the elbow.

"Wonderful." Her blink stalled a second longer than usual. Beyond knowing it took a bigger effort for her to be here tonight, she looked the same as always. "Jill says you've been a wonderful help."

We'd already had this conversation, so she was saying it for Jill's benefit. "I helped where I could."

"The room looks great." My dad barely took his eyes off Mom. I used to get annoyed by them making lovey-dovey faces at each other. He was there for her every second she needed, and the seconds she said she didn't need him. Leaving me to do more at the print shop. This was going to be hard to share the news about the interview. Even if I didn't get the job in Madison, they deserved to know I was looking.

Mom pointedly looked my way. "Ed Farinski is retiring."

I nodded back. All night I'd been nodding in conversations like this.

"Leaving an opening in administration." Jill's decorated Santa sweater demanded attention. It was like a homing beacon I couldn't look away from. "The requirement is a bachelor's in a business field and experience with city events."

I nodded some more. "Cool."

Mom's smile shifted. "A great opening for someone familiar with Crystal Cove who might be looking for a new opportunity."

They were all three watching for my reaction. "Me? Working for the mayor's office? Sounds like a conflict of interest." Never mind the conflict. I had zero interest working in the mayor's office.

Mom smiled at a guest walking past. "You'd have to apply for the job, of course. Jill and the other staff would handle the interview."

"You've been a huge help, Nick," Jill said. The glittering Santa on her sweater danced in agreement.

Someone had to be putting her up to this. "I'd say you're welcome, but you know I botched the planning. If it hadn't been for Megan, we wouldn't have even half of these decorations."

"Who is Megan?" Mom asked.

Jill responded with a careful smile. "Nick's friend, right?" She watched for my reaction.

Mom perked up. "I've been out of the loop. Is your friend here tonight?"

"Unfortunately, no. She's with her family and—" I stopped mid-sentence. Flies had open access to buzz into my mouth. Across the room, Megan stood by the front entrance in a red dress. She wore some kind of black cape with fur along the edges.

"Oh, I see," I heard Mom say as I brushed past her. "*Megan*."

I shifted around guests blocking my path and put myself in front of Megan. "You came." I tried limiting the wattage on my geeked state, but geek-beams shone bright like a disco light. Or, whatever. I was still thinking about dancing with Megan. How she fell into my arms. I loved every second of it.

She smiled and tugged at her cape. "Yeah. I'm not here alone though—"

"Nick."

Arms circled me and a hand clapped against my back. Diane Kreuger in for the big hug and Stu adding his method of affection. *Grin and bear it, dude.* "Thanks for coming out."

Megan half-covered her face with her hand. "Mom, lay off. You're scaring him."

Derek shook my hand. "Nick, good to see you again."

"Well, hello, Stu." Behind me, my own mother inserted herself into our space.

We were really doing this. Parents meeting my girl—no, not my girlfriend. "Mom, this is Megan. She's new to Stu Kreuger's family."

"Oh, how *wonderful*."

All the parents, including my dad now, exchanged greetings. My attention landed on Megan again and I shot her a sympathetic look. I guess I should have expected this to be awkward.

"My son has a check to contribute," Stu was saying as he held out an envelope. "He's sorry he couldn't be here tonight. He and his family had to leave early after the ham."

I snapped my fingers. "I heard the hog was a fifteen-pounder."

Megan laughed into her hand.

Dad gave me a puzzled look. "How on earth do you know how much their ham weighs?"

Mom nudged him and my cheeks lit up like...well, a Christmas tree, which was pretty freaking apt. I may as well pose for pictures and bust out the corsage.

Somehow sensing my thoughts, my mother nudged me toward Megan. "We should get you two in a picture." She waved the hired photographer over with her free hand. "We'd love some shots of these guests."

I mouthed *I'm sorry* to Megan. She only grinned. "It's okay. I expected this."

"And you still came?"

"My mom pulled the invitation off the fridge. Once she knew you and I were buddies, she suggested it herself."

I didn't like thinking of Megan as a *buddy*. Buddies went snowmobiling together. Megan...I wanted to share things with her. Share about myself. Share about life.

We were currently being maneuvered in front a fireplace at one end of the ballroom with a mantle decked out in boughs of holly and red ribbon—courtesy of Megan's efforts at the florist. The first photo included Stu, Diane, Derek, and Megan along with my family. Then both our mothers strategically cleared the family out, leaving Megan and me together. A corsage would have come in handy after all. At least it'd give me something to do with my hands.

"We should do a prom pose," Megan suggested, giggling. She stood with her back to me and placed my arms around her. "But hold your arms stiff. Pretend like you want to touch me but you're afraid."

My throat felt like a drained lake. "Sure." Pretend.

"Now smile really awkward."

I did as commanded and the photographer snapped away. Derek laughed.

"Now do a nice one," one of the mothers said. Honestly, I didn't know which one. Their combined powers were startling.

After the photographer moved on, Megan collapsed into laughs. "This is the face I made." She showed me a toothy frozen smile with dead eyes.

I cracked up. "Even if you're trying to look bad, you can't."

She swatted me. "Stop. Hey, is there something I can volunteer for? I don't have any cash to donate."

"You're a guest here. You don't have to spend any money."

"But it's a charity event."

"You've already done so much." I didn't want to be talking about this. There had to be some mistletoe around here. I should start carrying it with me.

"Excuse me, Nick Bennington?" An aging man in a red sweater vest held out his hand.

We shook. "Mr. Farinski. Heard you're retiring."

He adjusted his wire frame glasses. "It's time. You'll make a great replacement. Crystal Cove needs to keep tradition with a Bennington on staff."

I laughed a little too loud and cleared my throat. "Let's not get ahead of ourselves."

"You're a sharp kid and just what this town needs. We have an interview spot saved for you." He gave me a wink before moving on.

By some miracle, maybe Megan hadn't heard any of our conversation.

Megan inched closer. "What was that about keeping a Bennington on staff?"

No miracle for me. I backed us toward a corner, hoping to keep out of sight of, well, anybody. "It's nothing. This town, it's...small."

Megan squared off with me, her red dress like a stop sign I couldn't blow past. "Are you—" She stopped, seeming to consider her words. "I know I've meddled enough with your life, but I have to ask. What about the interview in Madison?"

"What interview in Madison?" That would be Mayor Bennington now at my side. I hadn't made our corner hidden enough.

"Hey, Mom." I flashed her my charming smile.

"What's in Madison?" she repeated. The smile never worked on her.

I ran a hand through my hair. "Nothing. Just..."

That feeling, when a parent waited to throw down the *gotcha* hammer and you had to do everything to delay the final slam? That was happening right now.

Megan gave me an encouraging smile.

"Nick," Mom urged.

"There's an interview. With Whitewater Distillery. For a marketing job."

Understanding crossed my mother's face. "That's what you meant about opportunity." Her expression landed somewhere neutral. "It sounds promising. Let me guess. Megan, you live in Madison?"

Megan's brow furrowed, then she shook her head no. "Chicago."

Mom pressed her lips together. "I'm sure you'll have more details for us. Nick, I came to tell you it's time to announce the first raffle winner."

I nodded as Mom walked away.

Megan ran her hand up my sleeve. "You talk about feeling held back, but the only person I see holding you back is yourself."

"It's just—" Just what? I was afraid to disappoint my family. No, more than that. I was...afraid. Life had a way of working out for me in

Crystal Cove. A new job opportunity practically handed to me. Even the Madison job wasn't much of a stretch. My parents wouldn't have to miss me at all since I'd still live in town. The real chance would be believing I could do it. To be someone outside of who I'd always been.

At the small stage, Jill held the microphone and announced the raffle winner. That was supposed to be me up there. "I can't talk about this now."

Right now, I needed to be Nick Bennington, mayor's son.

Chapter 14

Megan

I found Mom and Stu gathered at the edge of the crowd listening to raffle prize announcements and did my best to blend. The knee-length fitted red dress I borrowed from Stu's daughter fit surprisingly well and made me feel amazing. Stu's daughter and her family had planned to come to the benefit, but their kids were acting up and it quickly became a meltdown situation. Turned out even advanced degrees were no match for a three-year-old's tantrum and a five-year-old's refusal to wear pants.

I ended up really liking Stu's kids. After witnessing their struggle to manage the kids, they seemed fully human and less intimidating. The offer to borrow the dress made me even more encouraged about our future family events.

Less encouraging? Witnessing Nick freeze in front of his mom. Despite his declaration of feeling trapped here, he wasn't ready to leave Crystal Cove.

And it bothered me. Nick had dreams of doing more. Of being more than his family name. Didn't he want more?

Mom handed me a feathered mask and a Santa's Little Helper sign, beckoning me into the photo booth. I flashed a goofy grin, but it didn't feel as fun as earlier with Nick. Ugh, why was Nick holding himself back?

We emerged from the booth and waited for our pictures to print.

"Megan." Stu walked toward me. Alongside him, a woman with warm brown skin and curly natural hair approached. She wore a festive sprig of holly on her suit jacket lapel. "This is the associate dean of students at Boone College."

"Oh. Hello." I ripped off the feather eye mask and shook the woman's hand. "Nice to meet you."

"We're a small liberal arts college ten miles out from town," the woman explained.

Stu leaned in toward me. "She said it's easier than ever to transfer credits these days."

A numb sensation grew inside me. "That's...great. But I live in Chicago," I told the dean. "Kind of a long commute."

Mom laid a hand on my arm. "You could live with us while you commute. It would be temporary, until you finish your degree and get back on your feet."

"And when did I fall off my feet, exactly?" I asked my mom in a low tone. I kept up my smile for the dean.

"It's not easy making a living wage without a degree," Stu added. Ever the helpful suggester.

The dean looked between us, offering her own plastered-on smile. "We have flexible class schedules. You can continue to work and take courses. If that suits you." She handed me her business card.

This tension had to be unbearable for the dean. "Thank you. I'll think about it."

As the woman moved on, I turned to my mom. "I know you're trying to help, but putting me on the spot like that wasn't fair. I already told you I don't want to go back to college."

Mom winced. "Megan, we're only trying to help. To give you direction."

I didn't need direction. Okay, maybe a little focus wouldn't hurt, but the answer wasn't college. Not for me. "You're not helping. You're telling me who I am isn't enough." My voice trembled. If only red dresses bestowed the power to please parents who expected more.

"Honey, I'm sorry. I was thinking since you hit it off with Nick, it wouldn't be so bad to stay here with us. I thought maybe you'd look at life differently."

I could barely gather my thoughts fast enough. "Nick? You wanted to re-route my entire life because I hung out with a guy for a few days?" Not only was she re-arranging my career, but she wanted dibs on orchestrating my love life too? "I don't want to live in this nowhere town and go to some *stupid country college* nobody's heard of."

I sighed loudly and looked away from her. Not more than a few feet away, a Bennington's gaze zeroed in on me. Mayor Bennington's.

Apparently, the raffle was over and the mayor had freed herself for mingling. Beside her, Nick. Two Benningtons, both staring at me.

Chapter 15

Megan

I didn't need to be reminded I was a crap daughter for blasting my family in public and trashing the town along with a perfectly reputable rural liberal arts college. Every inch of my indelicate outburst replayed in my head. Sure, maybe not many people had overheard me, but the two who mattered most had.

I'd hurt Nick and his family on their own turf. Rushing over to them to explain and apologize, the mayor's frosty silence told me everything. Nick had offered a curt, *Let's talk later,* before steering his mother toward another group of guests.

My apology to Mom and Stu on the ride home from the benefit last night had been met with a simple request to talk more in the morning.

By the way: Merry Christmas.

"I'm sorry," I said at the breakfast table the following morning with Mom, Stu, and my brother.

Mom jammed a serving spoon into the steaming egg casserole in a red and green plaid dish. "I can't believe a daughter I raised has turned out so ungrateful." A hefty portion of casserole landed on Stu's coordinating plaid plate in a sloppy pile.

Stu directed a solemn look my way. "I think you owe Mayor Bennington an apology note. I have stationery in the den."

"Such inconsiderate rudeness is not tolerated in this family," Mom continued. "At *any* level. Megan Irene Campbell, you know better."

The middle name scorn cut deep. "I really am sorry. For embarrassing you and for belittling Crystal Cove." I held up my plate and silently accepted egg casserole. I moved the plate too soon and a chunk of sausage slimed onto the linen tablecloth, instantly releasing a grease stain.

"Did you talk to Nick?" Derek asked me quietly.

I shook my head no. I'd texted him an apology but didn't hear back. Probably best to cut ties, though I hadn't the heart to delete his number.

Mom let out a long, measured sigh. She steepled her hands over her plate. The Christmas tree-shaped block of butter displayed on a tiered serving tray waited for us to dig in, but no one did. "Megan, maybe you can share with us what you want out of life. That may help Stu and me to understand."

When my outburst wasn't playing like a highlight reel through my mind, I'd been thinking this over too. I thought back to my conversation with Nick. What did I love about living in the city? The arts, the culture, the things I often read about but missed in person because I worked so many hours and didn't have the funds for pricey ticketed events. I had, however, attended museum free days occasionally and even met up with one of our cafe regulars, Sadie, at the Chicago Historical Society. She became my unofficial tour guide for a fashion exhibit. Sadie worked her day job at a vintage shop. She did the retail hustle same as me while dreaming of running the shop and expanding the business online.

Only my something more was far more undefined.

"I like planning events," I blurted. I sounded ridiculous, and Mom and Stu's faltering, too-eager faces proved it. I swallowed. "I've been booking our musicians at the cafe and coordinating private events. I'm good at the planning. It's why I wanted the manager job at the cafe but..." I unfolded the red holly-trimmed fabric napkin and lay it across my lap, tugging at the edges. "I don't think manager is what I want. I think I want to run events. Like, as a job."

Derek finished chewing a forkful of egg scramble. "My company outsources our event planning. Even our holiday party. You can freelance that, you know."

"Freelancing isn't secure work." Stu looked at Mom while he said it.

"I know a lot of vendors." I ignored Stu's doubty-face. "People are always looking for space to use for events—it's how our cafe got into booking private parties. I have sources, I just need to better organize them." My thoughts sounded scattered, but ideas were coming together. "I never considered planning events myself outside of Drip."

Derek tapped his phone awake. "You could tag in with a company who already does event planning. Or start your own."

Mom pointed at Derek. "No phones at the table."

Stu held up a hand. "Let's take it easy on the starting your own business talk. Megan isn't in any position to start a company." He chuckled. "Not with an income making coffee drinks and an unreliable car with four bald tires."

Mom cast a stern look at her husband. "Stu. Please be mindful Megan is an adult and we aren't expected to direct her every move." Mom looked across the table at me. "I think knowing what you want to do is a great start. Even if you don't know how you'll go about it yet."

"All I'm saying," Stu went on, "is there are perfectly good full-time jobs with benefits at the manufacturing plant here in town. Megan can live here, we can help pay for college and—"

"*Stu.*" Mom's voice rose. "We're overstepping. Our role is to support. If Megan doesn't want to live with us and finish a degree, we can't make her." She looked at me. "I just want the best for you. I don't think I've trusted you enough that you have an idea what's best for yourself."

My heart tugged. "Thanks, Mom." She had my back and believed in my ability to dream for myself. "Your support means a lot."

Stu sat back. "I'm sorry if I've overstepped. Same as your mom, I want to see you happy."

I believed him. Watching Stu and my mom together, they looked happy. Content, even. Mom was smiling more than I'd seen her smile in years. "We're all family now. I appreciate how you care about my future. I really do. I'll even take you up on the tires, since it means that much to you."

Stu's face perked up. "I know a guy just outside of town. He'll give us a good deal on a full set of tires."

Mom's hand went to Stu's and she squeezed. Silent communication transferred between them and his expression softened.

"Thank you, Megan," Mom said. "We are a family. All of us here at this table."

My family. My suddenly-social-and-dancing-with-strangers-brother, my hardworking mom now in retirement, and a stepdad who got things right most of the time. His heart was in the right place. I'd never be like his kids, but I was realizing I didn't want to be like them. I wanted to be the best me.

Chapter 16

Nick

I'd made a mess of everything. What a doozy. *Ugh, dude, who says doozy?* No wonder Megan thought of me as some country bumpkin.

Christmas Day in the Bennington household included my brother home from college, three aunts, four uncles, five cousins, an infant and a toddler, grandparents, an old family friend, and of course my parents.

I was assigned potato peeling duty, which about summed up my standing at the moment.

I should have gone after Megan last night. Instead, I let her leave believing she'd hurt us. Well, she had—especially my mom. But I'd watched Stu pull the associate dean from Boone College over to Megan. Her stiff response as the conversation played out across the room from me signaled she might need support. I'd tried to get to her, but arrived at the worst possible time bringing with me the worst possible audience.

I wanted to tell Megan I'd never take a job in the mayor's office. Only I couldn't. I hadn't told my parents what I needed. That I didn't want life handed to me and I didn't want to stay trapped in a town that had my future planned out. Until I did that, how could I say anything to Megan?

Now here I was stuck in a house with every Bennington in the tri-county area.

"I heard your girlfriend made quite an impression." My grandma came up beside me at the kitchen counter. My Mom's mother. She gently released my hand from the potato peeler and took it from me. She grabbed a scrubbed-clean potato and flitted the tool across the skin with precision. "You never were good at this."

"She's not my girlfriend. She didn't mean to offend—it's complicated." I swept peel debris into the can for our compost. We were religious in our family about using food scraps for enriching soil. For winter, we kept a compost bin in the insulated pole barn.

"I'd like to meet her. I was sorry to miss the benefit last night. Believe me, I've heard an earful already."

My stomach sank. "About Megan?"

"Mmhmm. And about not going." Grandma smirked. At nearly eighty, the woman barcly had wrinkles. Her steel-gray hair made her look commanding, like a soldier. "Your mother gets worked up about social appearances. When I told her I was driving my friend Olga to our seniors' club party instead, she had a royal fit."

I kept my mouth shut. Mom and Grandma had some pretty famous feuds over the years, but they always turned out okay in the end. I'd learned to stay out of it.

"Here." She handed back the peeler. "Now do a better job. And tell me, why isn't this girl your girlfriend?"

I stumbled over a response and laughed instead. "Grandma, I know you want to see me fixed up, but she's only in town for the holiday. Her mom married Stu Krueger."

"Oh, how lovely. I recall his former wife working at the old florist shop on Main. The one the dry cleaners bought out."

Small towns. Everybody knew everyone and everything. "Sure."

"I don't want you fixed up with any trollop who comes your way."

Trollop? "Grandma, that word—"

She held up a finger. "Your mother seems riled-up about this girl helping with the event and bad-mouthing the town. I'm intrigued."

I clenched the peeler. "I'm sorry she put you in the middle. It's not like that."

Grandma washed more potatoes, silently placing them in the bowl to be peeled.

"See," I went on, "I got in over my head and Megan..." I told grandma everything. Finding Megan on the side of the road, trying to convince her to give me the tree, how inept I was at decorating fancy houses, and how we connected at Checkers. I skipped the kissing part, but sensed Grandma filled in those details. The lady had real power. I hadn't planned on telling her any of that.

"This Megan sounds like she challenges you. You're defending her, after all, even when your mother is dead set against saying this girl's name."

I rubbed my forehead. "After what Megan said, it makes sense Mom would be offended. But I think Mom also believes Megan is the reason I don't want the city job. She doesn't get I've been wanting to leave town before Megan showed up."

And that fell on me.

Grandma pointed to the large pot already on the stove indicating I should add the peeled potatoes. "You're a bright boy with so much heart. You don't have to stay in this town if you don't want."

"Thanks. But with Mom sick, you know I can't."

"She's doing well and has all of us." Grandma gestured toward the family room packed with relatives watching a holiday movie with the kids. Most of my family lived within ten or twenty miles. Only my brother lived farther, at Madison for college, same as I had.

Only unlike me, my brother applied for a post-grad internship in Minneapolis. Not for a second did he hesitate about moving over a five-hour drive away after college. Mom had looked at me when he told us his plans last night. I heard her look loud and clear. *I have you. My oldest boy stays.*

"I'll let her down," I told Grandma.

"Oh, pish. Saint Nick, I should call you." She rolled her eyes with the same intensity as my fourteen-year-old cousin. "If you're leaving to pursue a job you care about, how can you possibly let her down?"

Except, I hadn't gotten that far. I hadn't found an opportunity that *meant* something.

Grandma nudged me toward the family room. "You let me talk to your mother. I know how to handle her. Her survival rate is high and she caught the cancer early. Us Bennington's don't go down without a fight, and she's barely limping."

If Megan were here, I'd want her to meet Grandma. I wished she'd been at the benefit last night, but Grandma always lived life her own way.

Now it was time for me to live mine.

Chapter 17

Megan

New Year's Eve to me always signaled a fresh start. Dad was famous for using the previous year's wall calendar for kindling in our fireplace on New Year's Day. Couldn't get more symbolic than that to burn away the past.

Back on the schedule at Drip, I was working New Year's Eve as part of my bargain to get the days before Christmas off. Our largest party to date rented the cafe for New Year's Eve. I'd coordinated the rental and helped the customer arrange a blues and cover band, plus recommended a catering vendor. I was on-site to assist the hired staff with anything.

Part of me still hoped for a magical New Year's fantasy. A mysterious stranger sweeping me off my feet. A sudden call with my dream job on the other end. My next phase in life spelled out in glittery fireworks. Only I could barely glimpse the Navy Pier fireworks from the cafe two miles inland. The neighborhoods usually let off their own light shows, but they weren't exactly destiny-spelled-in-the-sky material.

This time of year was a dead zone for jobs. I'd been researching event planning and the companies in the area. I owed my coworkers a lot of shifts, so I couldn't quit Drip yet. Starting my own business sounded thrilling but terrifying. I could stay at the cafe and book events...but I already knew staying wouldn't satisfy me for too much longer.

When the party paused to count down the new year, I held my breath and made a wish.

The room exploded in cheers at the stroke of midnight.

Around me, couples kissed, friends embraced, and the band kicked back into gear with a classic Prince cover.

The calendar flipped over and my wish remained a wish. I was still alone.

I returned behind the coffee bar and tidied up. Was I really alone? I lived by myself, sure, but I had a family of co-workers. My friend Sadie invited me to an upcoming estate sale to hunt for treasures. My parents—yes, parents plural—loved me and were eager to visit Chicago as soon as the snow let up.

I couldn't help feeling down about blowing it with Nick. Then again, what would have come of us anyway? He wouldn't act on leaving his hometown and I only had interest to visit. As much as Crystal Cove dazzled me with lights and an excellent flat white, I hadn't been converted to a small town gal.

Still, his kiss remained imprinted on my lips.

Yes, silly conscience, it *was* stupid to hang magical New Year's hopes on a guy who probably right now danced with a girl home from college, kissing her under some mistletoe. Oh, you pesky mistletoe. How you betrayed me.

A solid truth settled in. My dreams were my responsibility. Whatever happened next had nothing to do with invented holiday magic. Fireworks weren't destiny. I made my own destiny.

One week later, my life changed. Sadie introduced me to a woman who owned a corporate event planning company in Lincoln Park. She needed part-time, temporary help while one of her staff went on maternity leave. I sent her my resume and we did an interview.

Despite my limited experience, since I could start right away and had excellent references, all I had to do now was say yes.

A real change. Another step toward discovering my capabilities.

I typed *yes* and hit send.

Another two weeks later, I slid my phone into my pocket and washed my hands in the break room before returning to the coffee bar. I was staying on at the café while I transitioned into work at the event planning company. Today, I had a nice long shift to look forward to on a zero-degree day with windchill dipping into the negatives. Store traffic would be slow. Time would tick even slower.

The door flew open and an icy gust of wind barreled in. A figure in a fur-lined hood stood letting the heat escape. A duffel bag hit the floor.

"Do you need help?" I circled out from the counter. "It's brutal out there."

The person—a guy—attempted to close the door, battling the fierce wind. Our shop didn't have a revolving door, which would have greatly helped reduce chilling wind gusts. Drip lived in an old building that soaked up a lot of money in regular maintenance of old pipes and drafty windows, with not much left for bigger improvements. Though maybe now with the added rental income, a new door could happen.

Something the next Drip manager could fix.

I pulled the door the rest of the way shut. A gloved hand rested on mine. I looked up and gasped. The face inside the hood was familiar but the setting all wrong. "Nick Bennington?"

Nick's smile lit his face. "You walk here from the train every day?"

"Today I drove. Too cold to walk."

His jaw hung. "You can park around here? I didn't think—I mean, I figured I had to take the El. I couldn't figure out the bus routes."

His gloved hand still covered mine, both of us holding the door closed. I slid my hand back to my side, stepping back. "Nick, what are you doing here?"

He tugged off his gloves and rubbed his hands together. "As of today, I live here."

"You...you do?" I couldn't have heard him right. "What happened to Madison? Or the town hall job?"

"Those jobs are still there. For somebody."

I couldn't speak. This was what speechless felt like.

He took in the empty cafe. "Are you the only one here?"

"Cam's in the back doing stock."

His focus moved to the chalkboard menu. "I'll take a flat white. I hear they're good."

I blinked. Of course. I worked here and Nick, a customer, actually wanted a warm drink on an insanely cold January day. I wiped my already dry hands against my apron and started for the counter.

"Megan." Nick moved toward me. His eyes sparkled the same pine green as they had over Christmas.

For some reason that surprised me, how the green shimmered as vibrantly here as it did in Crystal Cove. In my weird mind, Nick existed in a small town snow globe apart from my daily reality. Yet, here he stood in front of me now. In my reality.

"You don't have to make me a drink. I came here to see you."

I shoved my hands into the apron's front pocket. "You did?"

He laughed almost in a whisper. "Or you could say I happened to be in the neighborhood. Trudging through a blizzard on foot with a week's worth of clothes, coincidentally finding you."

I nudged the duffel bag with my shoe. "This is all you brought?"

"For now. I'm sleeping on a buddy's couch. He's in Lincoln something. Not Lincoln Park."

"Lincoln Square?"

He snapped his fingers. "That's it. The company I'm trying to get in with is on the Golden Coast."

"You mean the Gold Coast neighborhood?"

He shook his head laughing. "Clearly, I have no idea what I'm doing." He showed me his phone. "This company is a start-up for green tech initiatives for businesses. I reduced waste and cost at our printing company the last two years with changes to our processes. I looked at the jobs in green consulting and pitched myself to this company. I'm basically an intern with no salary, but they said they don't take just anyone on. If things go well, it should lead to a paid position. The good thing about living back in Crystal Cove is all the money I've saved up that I can live on now. And I sold my truck."

The back room door opened and Cam walked out. "Megan, do you want your break?"

"Yes," I answered without looking back at her. Nick still held out the phone, so I took it and scrolled to the company home page. "This looks great, Nick." I handed back the phone. "You did it. You left Wisconsin."

"I did. Well, not Wisconsin." He took in the café, a slow smile settling in. "This is exciting."

"I can imagine." I remembered my first days living in Chicago, walking the neighborhood, scavenging thrift stores for end tables and cool knickknacks for my shared apartment. "This must be a big change. I can't believe you sold your truck. That was a nice truck."

"My dad's got a beater car I can use when I go back to visit. No big deal."

"It sounds like you have everything figured out." I hoped my sincerity came through. "I mean it. You gave this thought. You can totally manage without a car here. I can show you the website to figure out bus routes. Sometimes the bus is more direct than the El depending where you're coming from." Babbling. I was babbling.

"Megan." Nick's voice went soft again. "There's something I haven't sorted out. It's why I came here."

My mouth went dry. I begged hope not to set up camp. Tamped down any thoughts of magical life-changing declarations. He probably needed some local recommendations.

"You showed me I was drifting with no purpose. I didn't believe in myself enough to take a big step. You took your chance and look how far you've come."

I flipped a hand at the worn, mismatched chairs and tables dotting the uneven hardwood floor. "I'm a barista at a coffee shop."

"Come on. You took a chance living here. You're living life the way you want."

I needed to stop minimizing what I'd worked for. "Actually, I accepted a part-time job with an event planning company."

His face lit. "Really? That's fantastic. Congratulations." He reached toward me, then retracted his hand, still smiling. "You inspired me to do more. I knew this was a now or never moment, and I have you to thank for it."

I couldn't help the warm fuzzies floating through me. "Well, thanks. I'm glad you felt inspired."

He grasped my hands. "You inspire me. Megan, I think I'm falling for you."

A saucer clattered to the counter, sending a shock through me.

"Sorry!" Cam yelled. "Megan, you've been holding out on me. This isn't a customer at all."

Nick barely flinched. He looked at me with a deep intensity I hadn't seen from him until now.

I blinked back at him. "You're...you..."

"If you have room in your life for a privileged country boy, I'd like to see more of you."

Hope broke out the fireworks. My heart surged and tears sprang up.

"Say *yessss*."

Was that destiny? Or, more likely Cam at the coffee bar. "Yes," I said for the second time today. "Yes, to you, yes to new. Yes to whatever this becomes." I slid in closer.

Nick unearthed something green and mangled from his pocket. He dangled the crumpled item overhead. "Just in case."

"If you don't kiss him, I'm coming over there," Cam called.

I threw my arms around Nick's sturdy, tree-hauling body. "I've been threatened."

His eyes sparked with mischief. "Yeah? What do you want to do about it?"

I made a show of thinking this over. "Oh, I don't know. Your lips, my lips. Maybe they could meet."

He wasted no more time. He leaned in, his lips cool from the outside chill. All I wanted to do was warm them. I pressed in, sending my warmth and feeling heat spread through me. He ran a hand up my back, a gentle pressure, bringing me close.

Finally, I pulled back. "I still can't believe you're here."

"I'm here." His eyes searched mine, pleading, waiting for something.

I knew what he needed to hear. "I'm falling for you, too."

He looked at me fully, taking in my words. Taking in me. Every thread of my being wove hope inside me. Hope for what was to come.

Nick kept me close. "I like this arrangement. Let's fall together."

Want more romance?

Falling Into Place

To Aaron Stanek, Mia is the one who got away. Who he pushed away, ruining her sports agent career. As Mia aims to save her childhood camp, Aaron determines to clean up his misfit hockey team's reckless reputation. Working together may give everyone a second chance, and he'll do anything to get one with Mia.

Also By Stephanie J. Scott

About the Author

Stephanie J. Scott writes young adult and romance about characters who put their passions first. Her debut ALTERATIONS about a fashion-obsessed loner who reinvents herself was a Romance Writers of America RITA® award finalist. She enjoys dance fitness, everything cats, and has a slight obsession with Instagram. A Midwest girl at heart, she resides outside of Chicago with her tech-of-all-trades husband and fuzzy furbabies.

Subscribe to my newsletter at www.stephaniejscott.com

www.ingramcontent.com/pod-product-compliance
Lightning Source LLC
Chambersburg PA
CBHW071836190726
48292CB00005B/1791